THE PLACE OF GOLD

by Gordon Neil Stewart

ISBN: 978-0-6484928-3-2 Paperback
Publisher: Harry Stewart
Date of publication: 2020

Cover figure from "Bathurst, circa 1850" by Joseph Backler (1813-1895) in State Library of New South Wales.

CONTENTS

SYNOPSIS

This work of fiction is a story of mining in the newly discovered gold fields of New South Wales in the early 1850s told from the point of view of the miners. It observes the transition of Australia's primary economic activity from pastoralism to commerce and some of the first glimmerings of coordinated industrial action on the goldfields of Australia. It tells the tale of a group of assorted diggers of alluvial gold on the goldfields near Bathurst. The leader is Australian-born George Barton a younger son of a squatter and an experienced bushman, who throws off his class background to become a digger. Some of his mates are of genteel but murky background from England, women from the slums of London and a Cornishman with mining experience. After conflicts with government authorities, some of the miners succeed, most fail, and the book ends with the dispersal of the group following the exhaustion of the easily extractable gold in the area.

CHAPTER 1

It was a bright sunny morning in early spring, and the frost and fog had melted away. "A grand day" said Mr Palmer, the Sofala clergyman, as Morgan and White's four-horse coach rolled down William Street to the sound of wheels on gravel and the clatter of horses' hooves. He was returning to his living from Bathurst, where he had collected enough money to build a proper church at Sofala to replace the bark hut where services were hitherto held.

"Too right," said the young man sitting next to him. "It's good to be alive on a day like this." The green hills swept away to the purple horizon, the Italian blue sky was flecked with little cottonwool clouds and there was enough chill in the air for the young man to pull out his brandy flask and offer it to Mr Palmer.

"Have a swig?"

"No thank you," said Mr Palmer, coldly. Being a clergyman of the English church, he was partial to port, but not given to drinking spirits so early in the morning with strange young men, specially when they had the wild, independent look of the native born.

George Barton shrugged his shoulders, took a drink and then buttoned up his coat against the breeze as the coach splashed through the ford and the straining horses pulled it up the bank on the other side and set out on the road to Peel at a fast trot. As the coach crossed the river flats George turned and looked back at the township where it lay shimmering in the morning sun. He heaved a sigh of relief; at last he was free, with no one to tell him what to do and where to go, and now he was on his way to search for gold, to chase the nimble pennyweight on the banks of the Turon River.

His friends and relations told George, sometimes rather disap-
provingly, that he looked a typical Cornstalk. He was about six
feet high, with the Currency peculiarity of fair hair and blue
eyes, and was dressed in corded trousers held up by a wide red
sash, a blue bag coat, a white shirt and blue necktie, set off with
a cabbage tree hat and high black boots.

He was just past his twenty-first birthday, a true Currency lad,
for he was born in Bathurst, and hitherto most of his life was
spent on his father's sheep run in the Bogan, hundreds of miles
to the West. George could read and write well enough (there
was a copy of David Copperfield in his swag, which he used to
read aloud to the men in the hut, of evenings, at their request,
for they were mostly bad at letters) and he could calculate how
many pounds of wool would come off the back of a mob of
sheep, and how many acres there were within the boundary of a
run.

But he was essentially a practical fellow, a regular bushman, as
his sister-in-law and her family said, in a rather patronising way,
when they first met him. True, he had ridden horses since he
could walk, and from his earliest days mustered sheep and cattle, rounded up brumbies, hunted kangaroos and run down dingos, killing them from the saddle with a blow from his stirrup
iron. He could kill and draw a sheep or a steer, bake a damper,
patch his moleskins, build a hut out of timber and bark, fell
trees and construct a stockyard. At shearing he was with the
best, and also he could find his way about the bush by the lay of
the land, the way the creeks flowed, or by the sun and the stars.
But these days, he felt, at home anyhow, in some way and for
some unknown reason this was not considered good enough, although it earned him the grudging approval of the men's hut and
of the few Aborigines who still lived down by the creek.

George's mother died when he was a boy, over ten years ago,
and was buried in the little station cemetery hidden in a grove

of lignums on the hill behind the house. Ever since the family moved to Goonigal years ago Mrs Barton became more and more withdrawn into herself. The children were really brought up by Mary Farrell, the housekeeper who had been with the family since she joined it as an assigned servant in the days of the System.

To all practical purposes, in fact, Mary was the mother of the household. But after the two girls grew up and were married, she and her brother Dan, who was Mr Barton's overseer, purchased with their savings a bit of land in the wild country south of Bathurst, where they kept a few sheep and cattle and grew crops on the occasional stretch of flat ground. After his wife's death Mr Barton's health deteriorated. He finally became a broken man and sat all day on the veranda, and even the slightest movement set him panting and gasping for breath. He would go blue in the lips and complain of a pain in the chest. There was a doctor in the locality, a poor man with degrees from some good medical school in England, but who had a sad ravaged face and who always smelt of rum by mid-day.

He would have long conversations with Mr Barton, but never did much good for his patient's condition. As good a remedy as any, the old man found, were the Holloway's Pills, sent up from Sydney. They at least seemed to relieve the pain, anyhow for a while. It was at that period that Rolly, the elder brother, really took charge of the situation. He was a young man with self-reliance, initiative and resourcefulness.

He possessed a certain grim determination, a dogged consistency. Perhaps, too, he had the luck which was necessary to succeed in the Colony, particularly in the environment of the wide Western Plains. On the sheep run where his father had squatted illegally years ago he was granted a fourteen-year lease, and when it expired he had preferential rights to the land. This was sufficient to keep away any would-be small settlers, relations of the people who kept the three or four disreputable inns within a fifty-mile radius of Goonigal.

The shanties were the resort of shepherds, shearers and others who, after they passed a year working in isolation, loneliness and solitude in the bush, spent every penny on drink, and when their cheques were dissipated, emerged sullen, drink sodden and red eyed to stagger back to a lonely hut all but lost in the quiet bush. Here they watched sheep all day until the next year and the next bout of drinking.

No wonder they all ended as mad as hatters and so accustomed were they to the wild solitude that they preferred it to the company of people. "But the shanty, bad as it is, may not be such an evil after all," was Rolly's comment. "If the men saved up their money they would go away to closer settled areas and farm for themselves and we would have no labour."

George was shocked not so much by the cruelty as by the illogicality of the words.

"How much could they save out of twenty-five pounds a year? They wouldn't get far on that!"

Rolly ignored him. When he was crossed he never argued, but preferred to change the subject.

Rolly considered the general democratic and contrary attitudes of the station hands and their friends at the shanties was a good reason why the gentlemen settlers should stick together. Occasionally some of his friends would meet at Goonigal or one of the other homesteads and talk over local matters. Some of the landowners were English, some Anglo-Irish and some Scots from the Lowlands. After the brandy circulated for a while and it was nearly time to leave they would drink a loyal toast in honour of the most gracious Queen, as they put it, to testify their loyal respect for the august personage, and follow it with three loud cheers which echoed as far as the men's hut and even down to the Aborigines who lived in the humpies by the creek.

People should not be resentful of the gentlemen settlers, was Rolly's thought. Think of the things his father had put up with! Shepherds killed and sheep slaughtered, in the days when there was trouble with the Aborigines. There must have been some sort of retaliation, for he remembered as a boy seeing severed heads of Aborigines nailed to the uprights of the stockyard. The blacks kept away after that, and then a few more peaceable ones camped by the creek and did odd jobs around the place for rations and tobacco.

So by the time Rolly grew up no one worried any more about the Aborigines. There were plenty of other things to worry about, of course. Drought, flood, bushfires, dingos that killed the sheep, the scab that spread so fast in the flocks in the last ten years. They tried all sorts of remedies and some killed more sheep than the disease. But the tobacco and sulphur mixture seemed to have got the plague under control. Then came the depression of the 'Forties when the price of sheep went down to sixpence a head, with the run thrown in. The Bartons only survived because they boiled down half the flock and sold the tallow for export.

Then there were other problems, such as quarrels with neighbours over boundaries, the everlasting shortage of labour, the rows with the shearers, ranting roaring blades, difficult to handle, triple distilled democrats and equalitarians who took offence at anything you said and wanted to live better than the masters.

George found he didn't really begrudge Rolly his position. After all, he was the elder, and he ran things with determination and judgement which in the last few years made the Barton place a prosperous one. True, the seasons were good and after the slump of the 'Forties the price of wool went steadily up. Now every year at Goonigal they shore thirty thousand sheep and there were also about a thousand cattle on the run and a good hundred horses.

Every year the wool clip went down to Sydney in creaking bullock drays which often took a couple of months or more to make the journey. When the clip was sold there came back notice that a substantial sum was placed to the Barton credit at the Bank.

Two years previously Rolly, a fine upstanding young man with rather more determined features than his younger brother went off to Sydney with the woolclip and stayed there for three months. A letter came back to say that he was to be married; there was no time for the family to come down for the event and anyhow the match was most suitable. So in no time he returned up country with his bride.

Amelia was only twenty, ten years younger than her husband. She was gently brought up, and it was a brave action for the young bride to go far out into the bush into unknown conditions and where there were so few white women and most of those of dubious origin and not of her class. On the other hand, people said, it was after all the duty of a wife to follow her husband wherever he went. Anyhow she felt sure of her Rolly, and her father knew that the Bartons came from an excellent family in England, or At Home, as he always called it. So really it was a very good match, Rolly had a fine property of great potential wealth when the ridiculous land laws were sorted out, an excellent future and suitable connections.

Amelia, too, came from the best of backgrounds. Her father was a clergyman of the English church, a Canon, while one of her sisters was married to Mr Charles Mannering, the chief secretary of the Lands Department, and the other to Mr Alexander Smythe, who owned two or three big runs on the Monaro and lived in a fine house near Goulburn. They were the sort of people who were received at Government House.

Amelia's arrival at Goonigal soon saw some big changes, my word! Young, pretty, with a skin like silk, not yet spoiled by the Colonial sunshine, clever, determined, she soon had her husband where she wanted him, and the rest of the household under her control, too. She developed the rather arrogant poise of the young married woman who has attained a husband who not only satisfies her sensual requirements but also gives her the social position that comes from wealth and power. She was the queen of a fifty miles radius, and those neighbours sufficiently respectable to be invited to the homestead acknowledged her position.

She would say:

"George, don't you think you should change in the evening, instead of wearing those rough working clothes?"

And one day George heard her say to her husband:

"I can't tolerate those native girls about the house. They are quite repulsive. Anyhow, one good English servant can do the work of half a dozen."

So the Aborigine girls were sent back to the humpies and an English maid was brought up from Sydney with an Irish orphan girl to do the rough work, and a determined attack was made on the dust, fleas, mosquitos, flies and ants that had for so long dominated the house. Also, it was no longer good enough to illuminate the rooms at night with an old tin can filled with tallow, with a piece of string as a wick, which gave off a murky, smoky light. Now real candles, not tallow but wax, were needed for the drawing room. Meals were served properly, too, and proper meals. It was no longer just meat, damper and tea, for Amelia insisted on fowls and a milking cow, so there were eggs, butter and cheese, sometimes even green vegetables and occasionally a roast chicken.

As there was yet no clergyman in the district, Rolly took the habit, prompted by his wife, of reading prayers in the big room on Sunday morning, looking very handsome and sitting under the new framed print of Queen Victoria, recently brought out from England. The family and the servants attended. It was made evident to the half dozen men in the hut that they would be welcome, but the hard bitten equalitarians preferred to spend the time patching their moleskins and shirts, smoking a pipe of Barrett's twist or playing some plaintive convict tune on the Jew's harp.

So gradually as the supplies arrived the homestead became more the sort of place Amelia was accustomed to live in. There were China plates and tea cups, a silver tea pot, table napkins and even a piano. An elegant Grand Cottage piano, six and seven eighths octaves, in a high finish walnut case, elegantly carried out, with massive truss legs and a shell front. A symbol, in fact, of the family's high social level. It was the first piano in the district and people came from miles around merely to have a look at it and the more respectable were allowed to hear Amelia play.

So at last the old homestead, sited upon a sandy ridge above flood level with the timber cut down around it and the grass burned off, began to have a new air, a more imposing presence. In his slow way George began to feel uncomfortable in these altered surroundings. Even more so when about a year after her marriage Amelia went off to Bathurst to stay with Rolly's sister, Ann, who was married to Mr Henry Lewis, the manager of the Bank in that town. She stayed there for the last month of her pregnancy. The confinement was successful, thanks to the jovial and respected Dr M'Cattie and Rolly found himself the father of a healthy son.

A year later the event was repeated and the son was joined by a daughter. This was in May 1851, and when Rolly went down to Bathurst and brought Amelia back to Goonigal he had some astonishing news; gold was discovered in a creek in the hills that had been named Ophir.

"Bathurst is quite mad!" said Amelia. "All sorts of disreputable people have flocked up from Sydney."

Every day, she said, parties went along the track now named the Ophir Road to Summerhill Creek. Mr Green, the Land Commissioner, was put in charge of the goldfield and was trying to keep order.

"Everybody," said Amelia, "Everybody supposes that the discovery will be followed by the dissolution of all the bonds of society, the annulment of law and order, and that rascality and chaos will inevitably hold sway."

Mr Deas Thomson, the Colonial Secretary, toured the area and was gone back to Sydney to advise the Governor on what to do. And now shepherds and other servants were leaving their masters to look for gold, for it was said that a fortune might be sometimes picked up in a creek bed.

Soon the news of the gold rush spread to the Bogan. Men began to drift off the sheep runs, leaving their masters to curse them and without avail invoke the Master and Servant Act. Later a few unsuccessful diggers drifted back, but the fact became widely known that an ordinary working man could make wages and often more on the goldfields. Thus he would become independent of the settlers and no longer have to follow sheep in the wild and lonely plains where it was likely he would scarcely see another face for months on end. This led to a terrible spirit of discontent with established ways, and even more so when diggings were opened up on an even bigger scale in the Port Phillip District and it became apparent that the whole nature of the country was changing. As a result of the shortage of labour and the independence of the common people, masters were seen driving their own drays and ladies of respectability were often obliged to cook the family dinner.

Rolly and Amelia were very indignant. They did not know which way to look for reliable labour. Then Mrs Lewis wrote from Bathurst to say that Mr Icily had brought thirty coolies from China to work on his estate at Coombing Park and this could well be the way to solve the problem. Also Mr Fitzgerald, the member of the Legislative Assembly who owned a number of sheep runs, dismissed all his white labour and brought in more than eighty coolies who were said to be less costly and more obedient. Captain Townsend sent ships regularly from Sydney to China and brought back loads of Celestials who could be hired from on board the vessel and paid a pittance and their rations. Soon gangs of coolies, dressed in wide trousers and short jackets with big straw hats on their heads and carrying their bundles on the ends of long poles, came up at a shuffling pace from Sydney and over the Blue Mountains to the most distant outback stations. None could speak English; they could only chatter in their own incomprehensible language. They were said to be very hard working, wanting nothing more than shelter, a little food and a blanket.

Old Mr Barton, sitting in the shade of the veranda, grumbled about the labour problem and talked of the good old days of assigned servants, when you could send a fellow off to the magistrate for a baker's dozen if he was lazy or insolent.

But George always got on well with the men. Rolly would work out that so and so needed doing and George would go down to the men's hut where he would find a couple sitting on their haunches in the dust chewing straws, and he would nod and say: "G'day" and they would say "G'day" and he would say: "My word, there's a mob of cleanskins down along the back creek and we'd better muster them up here, this morning, for branding."

And the men would nod and go off and saddle their horses and

George would saddle his, old Polly, a real do-or-dier, who never tired, and off they would go. Midday, they'd boil the billy and eat a bit of meat and damper and then bring the cattle back to the yards and work until dark, or until the work was finished. George knew the men would follow him and work hard because he was as good a bushmen as they were, or even better, and worked just as hard. Rolly was good, too, and the men respected him, but he had an aloofness which had grown particularly since his marriage. He was undoubtably the master and sometimes would show it.

As time passed George began to feel uncomfortable. Wasn't it time he was out on his own? He couldn't go on for ever being an unpaid overseer for his brother. One day he went to his father and told him what he thought about things.

"Of course, lad," said Mr Barton. "You know the property will go to Rolly as he's the elder. There'll be some money for you later but we haven't got enough to set you up on your own. Take a few cattle if you like and go out West and see what you can do. You might go overlanding for a while."

George nodded and went away to think things over. Did he but know it he was infected with the general unrest that spread across the Colony after the discovery of gold; the feeling that the old ways were ending, that something new and big was on the march.

Nevertheless, to go out West appealed to him, for the lonely isolated life, the endless open plains, the droughts, the bushfires, the floods, were things he was accustomed to since childhood. But at his young age he would like to see something of the world of men. An idea struck him. What about the goldfields? Why not try his luck there? That evening at dinner when they were in the big room drinking tea out of the china service, he said:

"My word, I thought I might go off to the diggings on the Turon and try me luck there for a while."

For a moment there was a stunned silence and then was there in-dignation! Rolly said the station was already short-handed and men were hard to get because of the gold, and he didn't know how he would manage if George went away. Amelia was indig-nant too and quite worked up.

"But, my dear George," she said. "The goldfields are full of ruffians and republicans and you might get murdered in your bed. The Turon is no place for a gentleman. And what do you know about gold digging?"

George shrugged his shoulders. He didn't quite know how one felt like a gentleman. He also considered that if shepherds and shearers could learn how to dig for gold, so could he, too. However, his father stood up for him, saying that the boy had scarcely ever been away from Goonigal since he was grown up and he ought to have a chance to see a bit of the world. The old man said:

"There's a market for beef in Bathurst with all the people who've come there, and prices are good. The lad can take some beasts down to the saleyard and stay with his sister for a sort of a holi-day."

"But not until the shearing's over!" cried Amelia.

"Good enough," answered old Mr Barton. "And he can stay with Mr Lewis and Ann until Christmas and then go and have a look at the diggings, if it amuses him."

And so it was agreed. As soon as the shearing was over George was off, with a man and a couple of dogs to help him with the cattle.

And off they went at the old jig jog and a packhorse trailing along behind to carry the gear. Old Joseph was George's companion, a real old hand who had come out in chains years ago and while a good one with cattle and sheep was still too weary to leave Goonigal for the hazards of the outside world.

They pushed the cattle slowly along the wild bush track, doing no more than ten or twelve miles a day, so the animals would be in good condition when they arrived at the
Bathurst saleyards. Now and then they passed lonely bush habitations where hollow-eyed women watched them from bark huts and wild children ran away into the scrub in fear at the sight of them.

Occasionally they paused for a noggin or two at some sly grog' shanty. Old Joseph would have rested longer but George was eager to be on the way, and he cut short the halts. The weather was fine and each night they slept in the open, by the fire, under the blazing stars, awakening at first light to watch the golden sun burst over the eastern horizon.

Sometimes as the sun came up and the dawn was all fresh and pearly, George would think what a wonderful and adventurous world he lived in: with a good, honest mate, a good horse, a couple of capable dogs and docile cattle. He was almost disappointed when at last they came down the big hill to see the red brick houses of Bathurst spread out on the plain below.

CHAPTER 2

Eliza King was born in Sheldon Street. It was a back alley near the Seven Dials district of London and she lived in one of a little row of houses that fronted on to the blank wall of a warehouse.

She, her elder sister and her mother lived in the back first floor in one of the houses. Sometimes there was a man with her mother for a night or two or even longer. There was once a father, a cheerful, jolly fellow. She remembered him dimly but he had long since disappeared. Her mother died after a while and was buried by the Parish. To Eliza she was rather a vague memory, a woman who never said much, who accepted things as they came, be they drink, men or starvation. The house was three storeys high with two rooms on each floor and a base-ment where vagrants slept and a small backyard with a stinking privy. The other rooms were inhabited by people who shared the same characteristics of being poor, usually sick, often drunk and who sold flowers and vegetables in the streets, swept cross-ing and sometimes sewed cheap clothing for manufacturers. Some were London born, some Irish and there was an old Scots woman who made lace on an antique loom.

No one knew who owned the house but once a week a hard-faced man called to collect the rent. You had to pay on the nail or he wanted to know the reason why. And if you were a couple of weeks late there was no excuse and out you went into the street to sleep under bridges, in archways or if luck would have it to find asylum in a lodging house where you paid by the night. When Eliza's sister Alice reached the age of about fourteen she started going out in the evenings and not coming home until early in the morning. When Alice dressed for her evening out-ings she wore a merino gown with a crinoline, a brown cloak and a porkpie hat with a feather in it. She also acquired a young man who looked after her. He was a rough and muscular Cockney pickpocket, a couple of years older than Alice, and already well established on the prigging lay.

After the death of her mother Eliza found it dull to stay at home in the evenings and she took to accompanying Alice on her promenades. As soon as they arrived in the West End they would walk down the Haymarket and call at a tavern where Alice was known. "Two glasses of Mother's Ruin, me lad," she'd tell the barman, who would then place two glasses of gin before them.

Then they would have the same again, especially if it was a cold night, and then go out into the Haymarket and Alice would parade up and down under the gas lamps until a man spoke to her and she went off with him. The men were usually older, with top hats and frock coats and canes with silver nobs. Eliza knew well what her sister did with the men; she had seen her mother with the men she brought into the house. Thus life went on for a year or two. Alice had a fair amount of money from the men; some she gave to her pickpocket friend, some she spent on drink and a lot went on new clothes and trinkets. But somehow nothing was ever put away for a rainy day.

Then Alice fell ill with a fever and was in bed for a month and when she ventured out again as soon as there was an evening with a cool wind she would develop a terrible cough, so bad that men looked askance at her, doubled up, exhausted by the bouts. So times were hard. Eliza suggested to her sister that she should go out to the Haymarket, for old men often asked her to go with them. But Alice refused and instead sent her to pawn the clothes. When the clothes were gone and there was no more money in the house and they were threatened with eviction for not paying the rent, Eliza went around the streets looking in shop windows and wondering what to do next. One wet winter evening she stood outside a baker's shop, gazing at the fresh succulent loaves. The baker turned away for a moment and she slipped in through the door, snatched a loaf off a tray and darted out into the street, only to run into the arms of a respectable looking gentleman who seized hold of her.

The baker set up a cry of "Thief!" and soon a policeman appeared and took her through the dreary streets to a police station. There she was duly registered and put in a cell with a drunken old woman and some slatternly younger ones accused of theft or other crimes. But the place had its good points, thought Eliza, for it was warm and dry, and she was given some rough food, and the other creatures in the cell made quite a fuss of her, seeing she was so young. The next day she was taken to Bow Street and after a while she was put in the dock, where she could just look over the edge.

A man read out aloud that Eliza King was charged with the theft of a loaf of bread. The magistrate, a benign old man, asked why she had taken the loaf.

"Because I was hungry, Sir," she said.

The old gentleman then made a long discourse about resisting temptation and then said that he would not send her to prison because of her youth but as a punishment for stealing she should receive a whipping. And that afternoon, in the house of correction, with other children who had offended against the law, she was laid on a board and a man pulled up her skirt and pulled down her draws and with all the other men, including the benign magistrate, watching intently, she was given twelve strokes of the birch on her poor skinny buttocks. Justice having been done she was let go and she went back to Sheldon Street and Alice rubbed the weals with fat.

There was now a little money in the house, for Alice's pickpocket friend had just made a good haul in Regent Street. He gave Alice a couple of sovereigns which kept them for a week or two. By this time Alice was a little better in health and was able to go out again to the Haymarket. But her skin had an unhealthy transparency, she was thin and her eyes seemed to grow larger and more luminous. Sometimes she lay abed all day, too tired to move.

One day a man came calling on the people in Sheldon Street to persuade them to migrate to Australia.

"It's always summer there," he said. "Wages are high and there's plenty of work. There's a shortage of women, too, and girls soon find a husband."

He was a contractor's agent, sent to find people to fill a ship with subsidised migrants so that in the Antipodes gentlemen settlers would have men to tend the sheep and ladies would have female servants to do the housework.

Alice, usually so pliant and like her mother accustomed to taking life as it came, suddenly found some determination. Before her rose the vision of a new life, in a perpetual summer, perhaps married to a good man, living in a cottage with roses around the door. And Eliza growing up a good girl and not ending on the Haymarket as she would inevitably would if they remained in London.

So Alice made a mark on a document that said she was of respectable character and in good health and would be at the docks at a certain time on a certain date to go aboard a vessel bound for New South Wales.

*   *   *

It was a bitter cold day with a fine sleety rain. The two girls sat huddled amidships, wrapped in shawls, watching the heaving grey ocean, bleak, desolate and ruthless, coming down in great monstrous waves that broke in showers of spray over the bow. The girls sat there in the cold to get away even for a while from the stench and muddle of below decks. There were three classes/ on the vessel; cabin passengers who lived aloof in the poop and were rarely seen; the intermediate class who also paid for the passage and were occasionally seen on deck and lived in relative comfort. Then there were the migrants, the pauper refuse of the Mother Country, debilitated and scrofulous, shovelled out to be got rid of, in the hope that they might be of some use else-where. They paid nothing for their passage and got jolly little for it. The families and girls were on one deck, where long bunks in two tiers were used for sleeping and long tables and benches stretched the length of the deck.

The migrants were mostly from London, some English but many Irish Cockneys. The men were broken down labourers from the docks, touts of all kinds, thieves and pickpockets, some with wives and children. They were not very useful people but they served at least in making the work force more numerous and thus bringing down the cost of labour. There were a few unemployed artisans, people who usually stuck to-gether and tried to keep some sort of order and decency in the general muddle. The women were brought up in poverty and wearied with excessive childbearing, and the girls all called themselves servants or seamstresses; but most had been on the batter in the Haymarket or even in the dockside. There were a few innocent ones among them, wide eyed and appalled by the tales of vice and debauchery recounted by their fellow passen-gers.

They were the restless hopeless dregs of a giant city, the out-pourings of the poorhouses, a stagnant crowd of brutish people driven to the vessel like a mob of sheep, treated heartlessly by the officers and crew, sometimes stripped of their money and belongings, fed on wormy biscuits and rotten meat; for the first weeks until they got their sea legs lying helplessly in the 'tween-decks in the midst of their own vomit and excrement.

No sooner were they on the ocean than waves of epidemics swept the 'tweendecks. Measles, whooping cough and diarrhoea spread among the children. There was typhus among the adults and many who came aboard sick of some deep-rooted illness grew worse in the hard conditions and died. Sometimes whole families were obliterated, leaving a husband, a wife or perhaps a small child quite alone, while the rest of the family was tied up in canvas and slipped over the side of the ship to rot in the depths of the ocean.

The officers and sailors and single men among the passengers pursued the unattached women like tigers on the prowl. Alice was frequently taken off to one of the officers' cabins; here in return for her favours she got better food and rum, instead of the rotten salt pork and hard biscuit and stagnant water served to the migrants.

Day after day passed endlessly. The weather grew warmer, then colder. One day the ship anchored in a fine harbour and black men in boats came out to sell fruit to the people who could afford to buy. But a few days later the ship passed into the great grey southern ocean where vast surges seemed to overtop the masts as she wallowed in the hollows. However, the captain pressed on more sail for a quick voyage was a profitable one. So with hatches battened down and sails doubled reefed the ship plunged on, her decks awash, a tiny speck in the infinite ocean. Down below the migrants huddled in their bunks, sick and frightened, while the ship creaked and lurched and shuddered when the waves swept it from end to end. To Eliza the voyage was a terrible experience. Sheldon Street and the Haymarket at least had an air of permanency about them and she there knew many people, either shopkeepers, neighbours, people in bars and tavern, men who were clients of her sister. But on the ship the migrants were withdrawn and unco-operative, concerned only with their own survival or that of their families. From her bunk Eliza watched people fall sick and die, mothers nurse their sick children, consumptives lay groaning all night to expire when the watery dawn came. One day in the midst of a terrible storm when the vessel lost a mast and two seamen were washed overboard a woman said to her, above the roaring of the waves: "We're dead, you know, and in hell. We're not alive any more, we are in hell, being punished for our sins."

But nevertheless one day, about five months after the ship left the Thames, it sailed through the soaring entrance to Port Jackson. Oh, how glad everyone was! How happy they were to see the olive-green hills, the yellow beaches where gay little waves were breaking.

*　　　*　　　*

It was a fine day in April 1851, when the vessel tied up at the wharf. Some of the migrants had people to meet them, others were selected and taken away by employers who visited the ship in search of labour. Those who remained were taken to the barracks at the other end of the town where a collection of huts were reserved for families and unmarried females.

Alice and Eliza slipped ashore, their belongings tied up in two bundles. No one stopped them, although they knew their names were on some list or other, and soon they would be looked for. Both, however, disliked and feared people in authority, people who put your names on lists and who would be sure to send you to do something you didn't want to do. So like two little animals they scuttled down the gangplank and hurried into the crowded streets that lay behind the quay. The place looked like some shabby English town set down in some strange environment, they thought. The houses and people reminded them of London; only the weather was warm and the sun bright, casting dark shadows. Suddenly the sky clouded over and there was a rapid and vast downpour of rain as if someone had emptied a great bucket of water over the town. The girls sheltered in a doorway and watched the gutters fill to overflowing and the dusty streets turn into a stretch of muddy pools. Then just as suddenly the rain stopped, the sunshine returned and steam rose from the wet streets. The girls wandered about all day, brought some bread and cheese and ate it in a sort of park. They talked to various people; men with families just off the ship, girls with nowhere to go, single men looking for work. True, it was easy enough for single men to find labouring jobs, but there was not much in the way of work for women.

In the main street there was a clatter of horse drawn vehicles, carriages, gigs, cabs, drays and carts. On the footway were merchants and clerks, talleymen from the warehouses, farmers in town to sell their produce, bushmen down from the inland for a spree. Outside the taverns were crowds of people drinking and talking and smoking short black pipes, while piemen, muffin-men and pigstrotter men hawked their wares. Behind the town street, alleyways climbed up into The Rocks, where the girls found stinking lanes crowded with people, many already drunk, dirty, ugly and dissipated. The place reminded them too much of Seven Dials so they went back to the wider streets where the shops were filled with goods and there were smart hotels and theatres.

By this time they were down to a few pennies; what to do next? They started knocking on doors, asking for work. For a while they were unsuccessful and were turned away.

Finally, footsore and tired, they came to a discreet house and knocked on the door, which was opened by a middle aged but well-dressed woman.

"We're lookin' for work, Mam," said Alice. "Can you help us?"

"Can you do housework?" asked the woman.

"Oh, yes," said Alice. "At home I was a parlour maid in a big house in Belgrave Square and me sister here worked in the scullery."

The woman made no comment but invited them into the kitchen and gave them food. She looked at Alice with sharp eyes and said she would engage them both as servants. To Alice who was more than wise in the ways of the world it was obvious that the place was a brothel. But at least it meant food and shelter. It was inevitable, however, that Alice decided that being a servant was hard work for little money so with the encouragement of Madame Rose, as the lady was called, she was appointed to the same position as the other young ladies of the house, while Eliza continued to work in the kitchen. It was much like being in London, only quieter and neither of them drank so much Mother's Ruin and ate better food and put on a little weight and looked less wan.

Life went on fairly calmly for a while at College Street. It was a busy time with lots of ships in the harbour and many ships' officers (for Madame Rose never received common seamen) knocking at the door at all hours. Then there were settlers down from the country with pockets full of money, buying champagne for all and a steady flow of commercial gentlemen who liked the calm and discreet nature of Madam Rose's establishment.

There were four girls, each with a room of their own, and kept busy by the steady flow of customers. There was Mary Ward, Colonial born, with pretty blond hair and rosy cheeks, a snub nose and delightful fawn-like eyes, graceful in her movements, always elegant, with a charm that captured the clients. Then there was Margaret Devlin, as dark as Mary was fair, born in Cork, and who tended to get over excited with the drink. Ann Fox who had beautiful, regular features which in repose expressed sorrow and suffering, was a close friend of the fourth girl, Johanna Gascoigne, a girl with a soft pale face, deep blue eyes and fine chestnut hair.

The girls were well dressed, well groomed, with lots of ribbon and lace, perfumed and powdered, given to drinking with their clients, happy with the money they earned, even after Madam Rose had her share. But they were hardened with the mercenary life, accustomed to going to bed with all sorts of men, from nervous clerks in bed with a woman for the first time, to hardened old squatters whose experience ranged from the bush vices of bestiality and sodomy, to drunken Aborigine women and the station cook, and for whom the delights of College Street made an unusual change.

The girls, however, underneath the brassy exterior, were full of repressed affection and made a pet of Eliza.

Madam Rose was a well-built woman of about forty-five or fifty, always carefully dressed, with costly rings flashing on her fingers. She had her own rooms in the house to which the girls were never invited. She put Eliza in a cap and apron and taught her how to answer the door properly and how to speak to visitors. There was rarely trouble in the house but nevertheless in the kitchen each night a burly man with a face battered by many encounters, evidently accustomed to dealing with drunks and other obstreperous people, sat in a chair, drank pots of beer and ate bread and cheese. There was also a smart and well-dressed gentleman who called at the house two or three times a week and who was said by the girls to be Madam Rose's partner, and in view of the time he stayed in her private apartments, probably her lover, too.

There was an elderly man, a Mr Huntley, a successful merchant, who made an occasional visit to the College Street house. No one quite knew what Mr Huntley did; it was said that he owned houses and had an interest in a brewery or a distillery. However, it was certain that he had much money to spend on his pleasures. After his visits the girls used to laugh and giggle among themselves. When Eliza opened the front door to him he would pinch her cheeks, fondle her arms and say:

"How's my pretty girl today?"

This Eliza knew to be pure flattery, for she had no illusions about her beauty, even if since she came to the Colony her cheeks had filled out a little. But the old man's caresses made her uncomfortable; she disliked the look in his eyes and the way he licked his lips. One day Madam Rose came to her in a confidential manner and said that Mr Huntley would like her to go up to the bedroom with him. Eliza shook her head.

"But it will be good money for you, girl, perhaps even a pound. Mr Huntley is a very generous gentleman."

Eliza said nothing, for she didn't really know how to express her feelings, but she shook her head again.

"All right, my girl, you'll regret this," said Madam Rose. So one of the older girls was dispatched upstairs. When Eliza told her sister what had happened Alice was furious.

"It musn't happen. The old bitch!" she exclaimed.

The following week Mr Huntley arrived one afternoon before the other customers usually appeared. He had a little talk with Madam Rose in her own room and then went upstairs to one of the bedrooms. Madam Rose then came down to kitchen where Eliza was peeling potatoes.

"Now, Eliza, you go upstairs to the old gentleman, and no nonsense about it!" she said.

"I won't," said Eliza, turning red in the face.

But Madam Rose took her by the shoulders and then twisted her right arm behind her back. Eliza tried to pull herself away. At that moment Bill the Basher came in smelling of beer and went to Madam Rose's help. Then, attracted by the commotion,

Johanna and Margaret appeared and began to protest. In the pandemonium Eliza managed to slip out of the grasp of her two captors, ran madly down the hall and escaped through the front door, which she slammed behind her, and quickly disappeared in the maze of narrow streets that led down towards the harbour.

This was the last that College Street was to see of her, and again one of the older girls was sent up to Mr Huntley to see what could be done with him. A few days later a little grimy boy appeared at the kitchen door of the College Street house with a message or Alice. It was to say that Eliza was gone to the gold diggings, where she was engaged to work in a hotel.

CHAPTER 3

George was made welcome enough at his sister's home but with two young children and another on the way she was almost too busy to notice her younger brother, after the first day or so.

Like the Goonigal people she and her husband disapproved of his intention to go to the digging to work as a common digger. Mr Lewis who was busy at the bank from dawn to dusk because of the extra business resulting from the gold advised him to bring another mob of cattle and even some sheep from Goonigal, as the first lot fetched a good price and there was a steady demand. George said he would like to see the Turon first, although he'd stay a few days in Bathurst just to have a look around. He found it exciting to be in a real town for the first time since he was grown up. It was exciting to sleep in a real brick house, to see carts and drays pass along the streets and more people in half an hour than you'd encounter usually in a couple of months on the Bogan.

He took to wandering up and down George and William streets looking into the shop windows and even venturing into Barrack Lane where the girls standing in the little doorways smiled at him and said things that made him blush. The town was crowded with diggers. Some were on the way to the way to the Turon and others were passing south towards Victoria where big fields were opening up on the Ovens River.

The diggers he found rough horny-handed men who called no man sir or mister, accustomed to hard work and rough living, who came to town to enjoy themselves and this meant a bounteous application of Jamaica Cream and visits to the girls in Barrack Lane. A few of the diggers were native born, others were shepherds and shearers who had been in the country for a long time, and some were recent arrivals in the Colony. There were also many people in the town who had business connections with gold; people with no intention of acquiring gold by the sweat of their brow, but who hoped that by devious means gold would come into their possession. They were merchants from Sydney with products to sell, gold buyers, men seeking to launch speculations of various kinds, to buy or sell mining claims or to introduce someone to someone else whereby somebody could make a profit.

George, however, felt more at home with the rough diggers at the bar of the Royal Hotel. There he could yarn about the best place to stake a claim — Peek's Crossing, New Zealand Point, even Jew's Mountain. The debate went on endlessly until George felt he knew every part of the Turon, although he had never set foot there. He felt he should set out immediately for the golden gullies but the variety and strangeness of the town excited and attracted him. He spent an evening at Mr Ashton's circus — a bright sparkling affair with beautiful girls on horseback, good riders, clever jugglers and laughable clowns. It was an eye opener, something he'd never seen before. This gave him a taste for night life and the next evening he spent at Mr Davis' Theatre Royal to see the performance. The bright lights, the applause of the crowd, the heat, the ferment, he found strange and exciting.

Returning to his sister's home that evening in the bright moonlight he heard a hammering noise outside the goal. A gang of workmen were erecting a gallows. Next day a murderer was to be done over, one of the carpenters told him. Public hangings were a regular thing in Bathurst, the fellow said. Why, years ago, when he was a little fellow, he'd been taken by his parents to see ten convicts suffer the drop at this very place.

The next morning, impelled by a strange curiosity, George slipped out of the house early. A crowd was already gathered in front of the gallows, among it many women and children. Already drawn up were the mounted troopers under Captain

Battye and also the town police, the blue coated charlies, sober for once, for it was only eight in the morning, and in charge of the district police inspector, Major Wentworth.

Soon the goal gate clanged sadly open and out came the ashen faced and trembling prisoner, one Timothy Sullivan, the convicted murderer, held by the stern faced jailer and accompanied by the grim hangman, Mr Smith, and the town's Catholic priest, Father Keating, who read the burial service as he walked. Slowly the group mounted the scaffold, but quickly Mr Smith, anxious to be on the morning coach back to Sydney, adjusted the noose and pulled the level that sent the poor rogue to fall into empty space.

But a low moan went up from the crowd for Mr Smith had not done his work properly and made the rope too long with the result that Sullivan's head was almost jerked from his body and a fountain of blood from the severed jugular soaked the corpse. George shivered, a cloud went over the sun and the scene darkened and a cold wind blew down the wide streets raising a cloud of dust. He went into the Royal to comfort himself with a noggin. There were a few diggers there already, despite the early hour, but George was in no mood for conversation. Suddenly he found the town no longer gay and animated. There was a sour taste in his mouth. He drained the glass, went out and walked down to the Queen's Hotel where he booked an outside seat on the mail to Sofala that left next morning at eight.

*　　　*　　　*

George was dreaming to himself as the coach splashed through Winburndale Creek and began to climb the hill on the other side. The horses took the strain as the road climbed upward and once the top was reached trotted gaily down towards the village of Peel. Here there was a stop to change the horses and time for the passengers to visit the bar of the Shearers' Arms. By now the road was a mere bullock track; the horses heaving and straining to keep the coach out of the ruts and gluepots, while the driver kept his eyes skinned for tree trunks and logs in the path. It was nearly ten o'clock by the time the coach topped the hill at Mount Clear and once more the horses broke into a trot on the decline down to the next creek.

Then there was another stop at the inn at the foot of Mount Wyagdon. Now there was a real steep pinch and the men alighted to help the horses. It was strange country to George and he looked back towards Bathurst across the valleys and the rolling hills, a long vista that took ages to disappear over the horizon. How different and perhaps more exciting than the flat grey plains of the West!

At last the top of the hill was reached and they paused to give the horses a blow while those who had a flask took a swig or two to get their strength back after the long climb. From there the track went straight through to Green Wattle Flat. This was a scattered village of sorts with a few dusty tents and George could see the diggers sinking shafts in the red soil.

Then suddenly the road went steeply down. This was the precipitous descent into the Turon valley. At first the coach rattled through thick bush. Then as the ragged trees that clung to the mountainside flashed by, George heard a strange rumbling, rattling noise from the valley below. The coach came out from behind a sidling and there before the travellers lay the dark and deep valley that millions of years of erosion has scoured out of the earth's surface. At the bottom of the valley a river of bright yellow water ran between green banks. In the river which rushed and rippled over the stones, hundreds of men worked feverishly.

They were digging holes in the river flats and carrying the dirt to the river's edge, where they washed it in queer timber contraptions about three feet long and two feet high, that the men rocked like a cradle. These, in fact, were the famous cradles used in the Californian goldfields, which Hargraves had copied to find gold near Ophir, the first goldfield in Australia. Men were shovelling dirt into the cradles, pouring water on top, and agitating the contraption so the dirt and pebbles ran off, leaving the gold caught in riffles at the bottom.

And this is what the men in the river valley were doing avidly, feverishly, as if they were anxious to get the greatest amount of work done before the sun set over the austere hills to the west. At the bottom of the big hill, scattered along the river bank, was Sofala, the place of gold, centre of the golden Turon. For all that it was but a collection of rough timber houses with many tents and bark huts crowded between the she oaks. The coach rattled and slithered down the rutted road, past the cemetery and the race course, to stop with the horses in a lather outside the timber facade of the Sofala hotel. It was just two o'clock in the afternoon.

*   *   *

My word, the Turon was a rough place! There were probably eight or ten thousand people spread along its banks and in nearby creeks from Jew's Mountain to Tambaroora. They were a rough lot, indeed, thought George after he had mixed with them a little. Independent looking men who stared at you unceremoniously. They mostly wore fustian or moleskin trousers, stout boots, a blouse or a short shirt, sometimes blue, sometimes scarlet, a dirty cabbage tree hat and often a short black pipe stuck in their faces and looking as if they rarely washed. Most of them wore the moustache, a new fashion. There were many foreigners; Germans, French, Italians, some of whom told George how they left home because of some trouble in 1848 that he had never heard of. There were fair haired Swedes, Africans from Africa or perhaps freed slaves from the United States or free blackmen from the West Indies. Then there were the Californians who had dug for gold in 'Forty nine and who knew more about the business than anyone else on the field, except perhaps the Cornish.

The diggers were in the habit of working in parties, sometimes four, six or more, and they equally shared out the work and the winnings. And now there were the big men with money who knew how to organise sluicing operation and often employed wages men to do the work. Among this great crowd there were many good men and some bad ones, but those who came to work hard to find gold were sufficient in numbers and strength to keep the bad ones in their place. The diggers, in fact, were a pretty sensible collection of hard working people. And did they work! No slave could work harder than the digger in search of gold, working from dawn to dusk, often up to his thighs in water, with the pick or the shovel or the crowbar. The gold, in fact, was the master, and the digger was his slave.

No surprisingly there was a vast amount of drinking far into the night, and men started work with a glass of rum to keep out the damp for the brown liquid made you catch your breath but it soothed your aching limbs and taut muscles. Drink, a pipe of tobacco, plenty of rough food and a bet on toss ha'penny or euchre, all helped to sooth the diggers' spirits after a twelve hour day swinging a shovel or rocking a cradle. These were rough times and rough men and there was a flood of bad language that frightened Mr Palmer and his fellow clerics. The diggers had no time to go to church, for they were too busy looking for gold to spare a moment for the salvation of their souls. Indeed, Mr Palmer had a church built, and a few respectable people came there on a Sunday, but the vast mass was indifferent.

Sometimes Mr Piddington, the dissenting minister, would hold a service on Sundays on the river flat and collect a few listeners, usually women, but on the outskirts there would be drinking and card playing going on all the while, and occasionally fight. On a few of the diggers the clergy had an influence, but these were mainly the tired, the weary and those who felt that going to church was a facet of social respectability. For the Irish, of course, it was different; they were Catholics and went to mass, for this was part of being Irish, of retaining a link with the green isle. Only when Dr Lang visited the goldfield did a big crowd turn up, for he was popular with the diggers as he supported their cause and was opposed to the mutton lords who wanted to put them down.

This great crowd of rough work-a-day fellows, thought George, felt themselves to be free men, and they ignored the very existence of the masters. They considered it right, too, that they should be able to work in peace and quiet, and that their property and their wives and children, when they had any, should be untroubled. They preferred in the event of any disturbance to keep the law and order themselves, especially as the Commissioner's troopers were never there when they were needed. One day George saw an example of this. He was walking past Erskine Flat when he heard a commotion and on investigation he found a hang-dog looking fellow held by a couple of diggers. The man was pale with fright and showed the whites of his eyes like a cornered animal.

It seems he was found stealing in a tent. The digger's wife discovered him ransacking the belongings in search of hidden gold. When she called for help a couple of her husband's mates seized the man. As usual there wasn't a trooper in sight and the nearest was probably dead drunk in a sly grog tent. There was real indignation among the crowd and some people heatedly proposed that the fellow be drowned in the river or shot. But in the end common-sense prevailed, for there was plenty of rough common-sense among the diggers, so the thief was given a good drubbing with a half inch rope and let go to hobble off muttering into the bush.

*　　*　　*

Here gold was God! At home George was accustomed from childhood to the talk about sheep, the price of wool, the danger of scab, the problem of labour. But here it was gold from morn to night.

"What's the price of gold today?"

"Haven't you heard? There's a new dealer next to the Prince of Wales Hotel who gives a shilling an ounce over the regular price."

"Remember Sally Thomson? He's on twenty ounces a day at Spring Creek and making a fortune."

"And out on the Meroo they're picking up nuggets in the creeks!"

"Hey, did you hear that old Smith, the man with the mule, has been robbed at Palmer's Oakey?"

"See the Commissioner on his horse. A sour lookin' cove."

Gold, gold, gold! All day long the cradles rattled on the river flats while half through the night in hotels and sly grog shops gold was talked about in a babble of a dozen tongues. There was talk of great nuggets found by chance in some distant gulley. The Bonair nugget, for example, found by Murphy at Louisa Creek, that weighed three hundred and sixty ounces and sold in Sydney for eleven hundred and fifty pounds, the King of the Meroo that weighed fifty ounces, and the famous Kerr's Hundredweight. Anyone might find a nugget and retire for life, to a neat little cottage.

If gold was the main subject of conversation second came the Turon River. What a river! In the wilful way of Australian rivers it ran a banker or it didn't run at all. Its source was in the rugged sandstone crags by Capertee, haunt of the last wild Aborigines. Down it came along the wild, rugged valley, cascading over rapids and through quiet, deep pools said to be haunted by the bunyip. It flowed on past Sofala and Tambaroora and in good seasons made a mighty river where it joined the Macquarie, a river quite worthy of a respectable country. Then the waters went off to the Western Plains and were finally dissipated in vast reedy marches to emerged an enfeebled trickle to join with the Darling River.

The diggers considered that where the river was concerned Gold Almighty was conspiring against them. Every morning anxiously eyes were cast at the dawning sky and also at evening time the sunset caused conjecture as to what sort of weather the morrow might bring.

In the name of gold the peaceful valley, undisturbed for centuries save by the quiet Aborigine and the gentle kangaroo, was violently torn to shreds. Everywhere trees were massacred for firewood or to make tent poles; then pits were dug until there was scarcely a space between them. Great cuttings were excavated up and down the hills, while valleys were turned topsy-turvy and dams were built, races were cut along sidings to bring water for cradles and long tomes, or to scour out hundreds of tons of dirt which had been lying undisturbed for millions of years past.

Nondescript houses were built of rough timber and sheets of bark, or rougher tents consisting of canvas squares on timber frames were erected here and there, while over golden holes whips and windlasses were set up, surrounded by rough machinery. The valley in fact looked like a battlefield, and in this dilapidated, ravaged and desolate scene, the diggers looked like so many ragged soldiers, the vanguard of civilisation's thrust into the quiet bush. And, like other battlefields, the Turon had its casualties. Disease stalked through the valley, the product of its filth.

The hungry diggers ate meat in vast quantities and the butchers brought stock from all around to slaughter. All along the river sheep and cattle had their throats cut and were strung up on rough gallows. In gullies piles of intestines were thrown away to rot and decay under vast clouds of blowflies. Old hides were left to rot on fences and the heads of sheep and cattle with all the other unwanted bits of their poor carcasses were left in stinking heaps. And the diggers, being but poor mortals, working hard and drinking hard, performed their natural functions like any other creature. In the thirty miles of the valley occupied by the diggers and in the adjacent creeks, people could be seen at dusk or dawn squatting behind a tree or a hush or at the water's edge. Night cans were emptied into creeks and the quiet valley was filled not only with the noise of cradles but with a variety of un-savoury stink and dubious liquids that trickled down creeks to the river, from which as a result arose an unwholesome miasma.

And over everything were the ubiquitous blowflies that flew from offal heap to turd heap and then into some one's damper or salt meat or drown themselves in the billys of post and rail tea.

Brush them away as you could, the flies flew into your eyes and ears, even into your mouth if you kept it open long enough. If they found a cut on your hand the next day it would be alive with maggots. When the weather was dry and the river level fell diseases abounded and the diggers became ill with dys-entery, Colonial fever and other distempers and lay pale and sick in their humpies and tents, and the Turon's few doctors went around administering potions. And if the diggers had no confidence in the doctors, for well they might not, they dosed themselves with Holloways Pills well known, according to the advertisement, to cure anything from the ague to worms.

Sometimes the diggers were carried to the hospital built quite early with money given by the diggers and the traders. The place was filled with casualties, men with broken bones who had been caught under a slide of rock or earth, who had fallen down a shaft or who had perhaps been beaten in a brawl. One of the first permanent institutions set up at Sofala, about the same time as the racecourse, was the cemetery. They lay side by side on the hill above the town, and to the cemetery there was a constant procession almost every day, of rough coffins. Some were respectable processions with a hearse and a clergyman, others only a few men with a rough coffin on a country cart, sometimes only a coffin on a hand cart brought up from the hospital by the gravedigger, lowered into the grave without ceremony and hastily covered up.

For many there were no headstones, for how could you inscribe just Bill or Big Pat or some such name, for that was all the deceased was known as, and his private papers if any, gave no further clue.

Such was the golden Turon where men of all nations dug furiously in the river flats and washed the gold out of the excrement tainted water. And the gold brought riches to a few, minor success to a lot, a bare wage to many and to some the utmost disaster. But to the newly arrived, like George, the place looked full of hope and wild romance. Could he make his fortune? My word, he could try! Perhaps the work was hard but the reward could be good, and he was young, strong and hopeful.

He humped his belongings off the coach and looked around for some shelter. There, in front of him, was the Pick and Shovel inn. He found the host, a beetle browed, hangdog sort of man, unwashed and shaggy, who offered him a rough bed in a rougher room. In the dining room a rough dinner was served for the price of two shillings, and that George washed down with rum, while he was waited on by the host's bedraggled wife.

*　　　*　　　*

For a day or two George wandered about the river flats watching how the diggers worked and talking to some of the more friendly and less busy ones. A licence was needed to dig for gold so he went up to the Commissioner's camp and paid the exorbitant sum of thirty shillings for one. Then he met a disgruntled digger who had bottomed on a couple of duffers and had decided to go back to his farm on the Hawkesbury. He sold George his miner's kit for a sovereign - pick, shovel, crowbar, dish and cradle, all in reasonable condition. George took the pan and wandered across the river flats until he found an abandoned hole by the river's edge. He scraped up a shovelful of dirt from the hole, filled the dish with dirt and water and started on the half circular, half vertical movement that left the lighter material on the top while the heavier fell to the bottom. He threw out the pebbles and washed away the clay until all he had at the bottom of the dish was some sand. In it were two or three tiny yellow-red specs - the gold.

He panned a dozen dishes and was the possessor of perhaps a tenth of a pennyweight of gold. Not enough to pay wages, but a valuable schooling in the art of panning! But he couldn't work by himself and a party of four was the best team. The next step, then, was to find some mates and to take up the job seriously.

CHAPTER 4

Eliza ran down the hill from College Street into the narrow and smelly streets of the valley. It was already evening, the quick Australian dusk was turning to night, lights were springing up in the houses and curtains were being drawn across the windows. A little cold wind blew off the harbour and the dark mass of the opposite shore was outlined against a pure sky in which the first stars were already shining. Here and there along the way women stood in lighted doorways, smiling at passing men, for there were many brothels in the district, brothels for poor men and sailors, not for the gentility and the respectable, as in College Street. That day three ships were arrived in Port Jackson and already a band of sailors, arm in arm, paraded the streets in search of comfort and pleasure.

Eliza wandered along, watching the people and wondering what she should do next. Food and shelter were necessary, for she wore only the thin dress in which she ran away from Madam Rosa's, and the nights grew cold now. Things might be worse, of course, for she had at least a pair of stockings and good shoes. But a start had to be made; she must eat.

So she went up to a group of sailors and plucked one by the arm, saying: "Give us a penny, mister, please." They were rough, hard men, tanned by the tropic sun, eager for food, drink and women. One, in a generous mood, gave her a bright sixpence, but another began to fondle her shoulder in a too familiar manner, so she ran off down the street. She managed to beg a couple more pennies from sailors, so she bought a hot pie off a stall and ate in the street. Then she slipped into a bar and paid fourpence for a dram of rum to warm her up. By now night was well and truly fallen and the streets were thick with people. Outside taverns men and women were gathered, shouting, drinking and singing, their faces livid masks in the garish light.

Eliza stumbled across a woman lying drunk in the gutter and already drunken men were stretched out on the pavement. In one place a preacher stood on a box and exhorted people to come to the Lord and give up the demon drink. One pale faced woman shouted at him: "Leave us alone, we know we are going to hell." Hanging around the outskirts of the crowd were many girls, some only children, who would accost men and go off with them. There were a few boys who did the same. A sailor asked Eliza to go with him for five shillings. Five shillings! A fortune to her at that moment. However, she refused and he swore at her. Why did she refuse, she asked herself? Perhaps because her sister told her she mustn't go with men until she was older - in fact not at all, if she had any sense, until she found a man who would marry her or at least keep her properly. Eliza remembered how Alice, who had lain with hundreds of men, told her how much she regretted the occupation, that girls in her trade either took to drink, became diseased or in some other way came to a bad end.

"Don't go on the batter," she once told Eliza. "Don't, whatever you do."

But it was not all that easy. Honest work was paid only a pittance and respectable women sneered at you while their husbands and brothers made propositions to you on the quiet. Why not just go to hell, as she heard the woman say earlier in the evening?

But something inside Eliza's head told her that there might still yet be hope, that there was perhaps a way out, that one should not give in. There were an awful lot of things in life better than lying with a multitude of men, young or old, drunk or sober, smelly or clean. Eliza slipped into the tavern and bought another noggin with the last of her money. At least it would help to keep warm for a while, for the night was growing cold and the wind cooler. Where would she go? At least drunken sailors and the prostitutes and other miserable people who lived in the 'Loo had some sort of shelter and warmth, and some sort of companionship, someone to snuggle up to for comfort, and even a bed to lie in.

She wandered through the dark streets. As the time passed there were less and less people to be seen. For respectable citizens it was dangerous to be about but the sinister men who lurked in back alleys showed no interest in destitute waifs. At last she found a pile of empty barrels. Some were already occupied by people with no other home. Nearby were some sacks. Eliza picked up a couple and then found a stray cat. with the cat in her arms she curled up on one sack and drew the other over her. The cat, a weary little tabby, began to purr and licked her cheek. At last she fell asleep.

*   *   *

The next morning she awoke at dawn, stiff and cramped. The cat mewed at her and skipped off in search of a breakfast. Eliza crawled out of her shelter and washed her face and hands under a pump. Smoothing her dress and hair with her hands she set off through the early morning streets to find if it was possible for an honest girl to earn a living in Sydney town.

At Madam Rose's she was told that in town there were agencies that found employment for servant girls, for with the gold rush turmoil there was a terrible shortage of servant girls. Perhaps she might be able to find work even of the most humble kind. In Pitt Street she found a registry for servants but it was still closed, so she wandered about the town for an hour or so.

Then she went back to the registry where a pert young woman asked her some questions and they told her she had no work for waifs and strays. Eliza tried another registry with the same result. She sighed, for by now she was tired and hungry. One more try, and perhaps the third time would be lucky. In the office was a rough looking man with an equally rough looking wife. They wanted a general servant for hotel work on the goldfields, to whence they were going that very afternoon, in a loaded dray that stood outside in the street.

"Four shillings a week and keep," said the man. "And you'll undertake to stay three years."

What else to do? Eliza agreed to the wage and asked for an advance with which to buy herself a coat, for it was said to be cold in the mountains, for sure. Grudgingly she was given ten shillings by the grim faced woman. Watched, to see that she did not run off, she bought a coat for six shillings and a pair of thick stockings. Then she paid a little grimy boy the sum of three pence to take a message to her sister to say that she was gone to work in the goldfields at a place called Sofala. So off they set along the Parramatta Road with the mistress sitting in the dray, the master leading the horse and Eliza walking by his side.

Mr and Mrs Weston, for that was their name, were from London, come to Australia as free settlers some time before the gold rush. For some years they had kept a tavern near Darling Harbour. Mr Weston was tall and heavy as becomes a publican, with a droopy moustache and big hands like a bunch of sausages. He must have been about forty and Mrs Weston, a short woman with a thick and powerful figure, was a little younger. Both had flushed, red faces, both had hard, accusing eyes.

News came from the goldfields that there was big money to be made in catering for the diggers' needs, so they sold their tavern and decided to set up a hotel at Sofala, the new, booming, turbulent centre of the goldfields. Then they purchased a horse and cart and filled the cart with the many articles needed to establish a hotel. The load was so heavy that the horse, a not very young screw necked bay, strained even to pull it up even a slight incline.

It was Mrs Weston's idea that they should find someone to help them, preferably young, and engaged in Sydney, for labour was scarce and expensive on the goldfields.

Along the dusty Parramatta Road they trudged with a grumpy grey old dog forming the fourth member of the party. Like his owners he had hard, suspicious eyes and refused to respond to the occasional gesture of friendship made to him by Eliza.

So far the road surface was good enough, sometimes shaded by clumps of eucalypts growing along the side. It was busy with traffic going to or from the goldfields, parties of men on foot, some in carts, even a party of Californians in a chartered coach, with red shirts, Californian hats, flowing moustaches and bowie knives and revolvers stuck in their belts.

By the time the Westons reached Parramatta the day was ending, so they took the cart to an unoccupied paddock where the horse was unharnessed and left to graze and Eliza was gruffly told to find some wood for the fire and cook the supper.

That night Eliza's bed was a blanket under the cart. The night was fine and she lay and looked at the everlasting stars roaring down at her from the black sky and listened to the horse munching the grass while her master and mistress snored away on a mattress on the cart. To the west she could see the line of the mountains looking mysterious and menacing. The tang of the grass tickled her nostrils as she nodded off to sleep.

Next morning they were up early and trudged on to the scattered huts of Penrith, then crossed the river on a punt. Then began the long pull up the mountain road where the horse sweated and strained and even Mrs Weston got off the cart and walked to give the poor beast some help. She limped along behind the cart grumbling to herself until her husband roughly told her to shut up. At last they reached the top of the range and

Eliza looked with wonder at the view of ridge upon ridge of tree covered mountain stretching to the horizon. Accustomed only to the dusty streets and houses of Sydney, she wondered what strange and dangerous animals and wild natives might be hiding menacingly in the endless forest.

When they camped for the night they had a visitor, a one-time patron of the Westons, on his way back to Sydney after making a pile on the Turon. The rum bottle was brought out and the trio yarned long into the night about the goldfields.

The mountain road was rutted and steep and busy with traffic. Once they saw the gold escort trot past on the way to Sydney, a smart four wheel vehicle with four horses and outriders in uniform, with an officer with a sword.

It was five weary days before they reached the Bathurst Plains and at last entered the town itself, a dusty little village of red brick buildings where herds of goats and packs of savage dogs wandered through the streets. They camped by the river while Weston went off to talk business with people; something to do with obtaining a licence, Mrs Weston said.

Already Eliza had sized up her employers. They were both people keen about money and determined to make as much as possible in the only way they knew - selling food and drink. Weston was a rough enough fellow, capable of dealing with unruly customers, forceful but ignorant. His wife, however, was the one who counted the pennies, who calculated where the most profitable ventures lay, who knew how to buy in the cheapest market and sell in the dearest, who really had a shrewd eye for business. They were both hard workers, who would work until they dropped and then count the takings and put them in an old sock under the mattress.

Their relationship was not based as much on affection as upon common interest. The only thing, thought Eliza, for which they had any real interest was the old dog, for whom they chose the best cuts of meat. He would sit by Mrs Weston and look deeply into her eyes and she would occasionally pat him on the head. The only time when Eliza noticed the Westons show any emotion was when a big black dog seized old Fido, as he was called, by the leg, and Weston beat him off with a length of wood and he ran away howling.

After a couple of days in Bathurst they set off along the rough road to the Turon. Then they came to a high escarpment. There was an inn at the bottom of the pinch where the publican advised Weston to take his load up in two parts, so Eliza was left to guard the half remaining at the bottom of the hill, while the husband and wife urged the weary horse up the steep and rutted track. Eliza watched them crawl up the hill, like a fly up a wall, with Weston flogging the horse every inch of the way. Hours later Weston returned, but the horse was so exhausted that they could not start off again until the next morning.

Finally they arrived at Sofala and then for days it was work from dawn to dusk. A builder went to work on the new hotel, timber was hauled from the hills, slabs were cut for the walls and sheets of bark were laid on the rafters to made the structure watertight.

At last Weston himself was able to nail up the sign – the Pick and Shovel Inn, a good name for a diggers' hostelry. The main room was the bar, and then the dining room, and there were a few rough bedrooms for any guests. A notice was put up: "Meals two shillings, rooms two shillings".

While Weston installed himself in the bar Mrs Western's preserve was the dining room. She knew what diggers wanted; good hot food and plenty of it. A big plate of soup, a dish of mutton or beef with lots of vegetables, finished off with a plate of plumb duff big enough to sink a ship. Just the meal for men who had been working like slaves all day perhaps with water up to their waists. The place was kept open until late at night, even on Sundays, although the clergyman were campaigning for Sunday closing, and at all hours hungry diggers came in to soak up with food the bellyful of rum they had consumed at the bar.

Eliza worked from before daylight until the last customer was gone, and then slept like a log on a pile of sacks in a skillion at the back of the hotel. It was her duty to rise first, light the fire, wake Mrs Weston, help with the breakfast, made the beds, peel potatoes, lay tables, serve meals, wash up and so on.

The plumpness she had acquired at Madam Rose's soon wore off and she was once again as thin as a rake. There were other workers at the hotel as well as Eliza; a barmaid all bosom and ribbons, a poor old man who cut wood for the fire and the occasional digger's wife who helped in the kitchen. They were all driven like slaves by Mrs Weston who worked as hard as anyone and who had a capacity for judging how many potatoes, how much meat, how much flour and other ingredients were needed for the next meal. She had the situation under control, too, and was always there to urge people on, telling them to hurry up, look sharp, do this, do that.

One day everything seemed to go wrong. The mutton was found to be flyblown. Half the potatoes were mouldy. The kitchen fire smoked and the woman Mrs Weston hired to do the cooking didn't arrive. The midday meal proved bad enough but the dinner was a disaster. The soup was cool, the meat undercooked. The diners began to grumble and one or two said they wouldn't come back next time. Mrs Weston's nerves were on edge and she had a vision of the takings falling off, and the diggers eating elsewhere, for they were temperamental where food was concerned.

Then Eliza, hurrying through the dining room, tripped over her feet and fell flat on her face, dropping a plate full of soup and splashing a customer. This to Mrs Weston was the last straw. As

Eliza struggled to her feet Mrs Weston gave her a thump on the ear and screamed: "Clean up that mess, you lazy Irish orphan bastard!"

While Eliza was a little hazy about her parentage there was one thing of which she was sure, and that was to call her lazy was ridiculous and highly unjust, seeing that she worked as hard as anyone from daybreak until after dusk. The injustice of the situation rankled so much that in a rage she picked up the plate and hit Mrs Weston on the head with it.

This caused some mirth among the diners, who had already taken Eliza's side and were unhappy with the service, anyhow. However, Mrs Weston clutched her head, called for her husband who, hearing the commotion, was already at the door, red faced and angry, and rushed at Eliza.

Flight was the only solution and Eliza ran rapidly out of the front door into the street and disappeared up a dark alley, where Mrs Weston soon lost sight of her.

CHAPTER 5

It was a bright day in early spring and the sun was warm enough for the diggers to throw off their coats and open their shirts. This is exactly what George was doing on the river flat near Green Point. He and his mates had four claims set together, which made an area four times sixty feet, carefully pegged and registered with the Commissioner.

The river was low and the aim was to dig down to find the washing stuff, get it out and separate the gold before rainy weather might bring a flood. The hole was already ten feet down and George, being a competent bush carpenter, had constructed a whip. This consisted of a length of timber held in the forked branch of a tree on a shaft, with a weight at one end and a raw hide bucket on a rope at the other. When the bucket was filled with dirt, the weight was depressed and the bucket came up out of the hole with the least effort.

The shaft was sunk six feet by six to give plenty of room. Above his head George could see a square of blue sky across which little pink cotton wool clouds sped gaily. He filled the bucket with dirt and called out "heave ho!" and Pat Ryan at the top of the shaft depressed the other end of the whip and the bucket rose in the air until Pat could grab hold and empty it on a heap of dirt waiting to be washed. George took up his pick to break some more dirt when Pat called to him "Tucker's up". Like the good workman he was, George cleaned up the remaining free dirt at the bottom of the shaft and placed his pick and shovel in a corner ready for his return. Then he clambered up the shaft and with Pat at his side walked over to the camp set about a hundred yards away on the river bank and above flood level.

*   *   *

After a week at the inn George felt it was time to set up on his own to dig for gold. One morning he had a talk with a sturdy young fellow camped by the river bank. He'd been working for wages with Captain Harris's party, for two pounds a week, he said, but he wanted something better and was looking around. He was native born, like George, and his name was Pat Ryan, and his parents had a small farm near O'Connell. Pat was not one who said much; like most of the native born he didn't waste words, but he looked a hard worker as his muscular arms testified. So he and George agreed to be mates. Now they wanted a couple more fellows to join them and the team would be complete, all ready to chase the nimble pennyweight.

Most diggers tended to stick together in their nationalities; the Irish with the Irish, the English with the English; the Scots, in particular, never worked with any but other Scots. This applied to the foreigners, too. The Californians worked in their own parties, as did the French, the Germans and the others. It was unusual to find a mixed party. But that didn't bother George. He was brought up a Protestant and he supposed Pat was a Catholic of sorts, being Irish, although he'd never been in a church.

In fact he could neither read nor write, had scarcely ever been in a town, thought an oath was one of the words you embellished your speech with and didn't know there was a governor in the Colony until he came to the Turon and saw Sir Charles Augustus FitzRoy on a black horse when he visited the diggings.

So far so good. But now it was time to find a place and peg a claim. They wandered upstream and by Erskine Flat came across a couple of new arrivals, real new chums, awkward looking fellows burned by the sun and English, by their accent. One was tall and fair, the other one short and dark.

"We're just off a ship," said the tall one, dumping his swag by the track. "Are we far from Sofala?" He spoke with a sort of forced joviality as if he was doing his best to talk to Pat and George as if they were his equals.

"We would like to go digging for gold," he said. "But having just arrived here, we don't really know how to go about it."

The tall one was named Harry Pole, it seemed. The shorter one, who had the look of a horseman about him, said he was usually called the Major. On the spur of the moment George asked them to join up with him and Pat, if they cared to put in a few notes to pay for their share of the plant. They agreed, seeming only too delighted to have someone who could show them the ropes. George told them to go to the Camp and pay for a licence each and they would all meet: in the town in the evening. So off they went, quite willing and cheerful.

The next step, then, was to find a good spot to peg a claim. In the bar of a Sofala inn a digger had mentioned to George that he should try farther up the river, and said that a place named Green Point was worth investigation, as he reckoned there was still some good ground there.

So George and Pat went on up the river past the Californians at Erskine Flat, who had turned the place upside down and sluiced away the whole side of the hill, over the ford at Big Oaky Creek and up Ration Hill. On the other side lay the huts of the village of Walberton. For a moment they considered pegging a claim somewhere along Pennyweight Creek, which ran off to the right into the hills, but there seemed too many people working there already, and the ground looked uncomfortably crowded.

On they went up Scabby Hill and at the summit turned to look back down the river towards Sofala. All along the river the smoke from the camp fires hung heavily in the air. On the north side the river was overhung by whinstone crags, covered with olive green eucalypts. At the bottom of the hill the track crossed the Turon at a rough ford and wondered off up through the bushy mountainous country to join the Mudgee road at Cherry Tree.

At the ford the river curved. This was Green Point. The right bank was high, but a wide expanse of gravel lay between it and the left bank, right against the green slopes of Scabby Hill. George already knew that the best claims were at river curves, usually about fifteen feet out from the bank, where the gold lay the richest in the sand and gravel.'

So this looked a likely spot and one could make the camp on the left bank well above high water mark. There not many claims being worked in the area and George said:

"Let's peg here," as if he had reason to think that multitude of golden nuggets nestled under his feet. Of course he hadn't the faintest idea whether the area good or not and he selected it by pure chance. And luck, good or bad, had a great deal to do with success at the diggings. After all one had to begin somewhere.

So George and Pat cut some stakes and pegged an area for a party of four, knocking the pegs in good and tight. There they were and there they be!

Back they went to Sofala and George took a few notes from his belt for he was to stake Pat who was a bit short of ready money. So he purchased a couple of buckets and pannikins, flour, candles, salt meat, two more picks and shovels and some tea. Now they were equipped.

The other two turned up that evening, all right, but they had both been worshipping the jolly god at the Pick and Shovel Inn; the Major to the extent that he couldn't stand up, while Harry Pole had great difficulty in moving in any direction without falling over. So the two sober ones bedded them down at Pat's camp and told them to keep an eye on the gear.

It was evening by this time and Pat and George went off to the Californian Restaurant for a meal and a noggin or two in the good old Colonial style. They arrived in the midst of a row and thought for a moment there would be trouble. Jolly old Louisa, the West Indian woman who did people's laundry, came in for a quick drink and sat down at a table where there were already two Californians. They started up, high faced, proud, indignant.

"We won't sit at the same table as this gadam nigra woman," one shouted and the other said he was going off to get his whip to give her a good thrashing same as he would to any uppity nigra woman back in Georgia. But there was a growl of protest from the diggers for Louisa was liked and there were too many among those present who had once been convict slates and known the shame of bondage and had been lashed themselves in the old days of the System. However, Louisa solved the problem by emptying her glass and slipping out of the door.

So then the diggers settled down to the serious business of eating and drinking. Here and there a group played cards and in a corner others played three up or heads and tails. So it went on far into the night, with a heavy consumption of Jamaica cream and a great concentration of tobacco smoke.

Early the next morning George and his party (for he seemed to be unconsciously accepted as the leading spirit) set off for Green Point. Pat, the youngest and strongest, carried the cradle on his back while the other three shared the gear between them.

It was dawn when the three men started, the pearly Australian dawn, the stars were gently fading in the sky and a soft wind blew from behind a bank of cloud. There was a mist on the river and the diggers here and there were stirring and the smoke from early fires drifted across the valley around the base of the great whinstone crags that stood out starkly against the morning sky. The water rustled gently over the stones and gurgled around the roots of the few casuarina trees that still stood, too misshapen and awkward even to be cut down for firewood, by the river's edge. Out of the dark mountains to the east the sun arose and a mob of kookaburras burst into mad laughter, while stern white cockatoos swooped over the travellers, screaming as if to warn the bush folk that more madmen were on the way to search for gold.

*   *   *

On the Turon there was unrest among the diggers. This existed from the beginning, as soon as the government attempted to impose some sort of control over the goldfields. The diggers, rough men that they were and avidly independent, felt that the control was not for their benefit, that the government was against them. And so it was! What would you expect, they said, when the government in Sydney was run by the sheep kings, the wool and mutton lords of the interior, who abhorred the discovery of gold because gold and the diggers disrupted their placid life, causing their shepherds and hut keepers to run away to seek their fortunes on the diggings.

And the king of the squatters was William Charles Wentworth. Wentworth! Once the great democrat, the man who talked once about freedom and democracy and independence and who now wanted to crush the diggers so they would go back to tailing sheep at twenty pounds a year on the great lonely and desolate plains of the outback.

As commissioner for the Western Goldfields the government in Sydney appointed a Mr Green who, as the Major was quick to point out, had the habitudes of an officer and a gentleman and was an autocrat by custom, education and circumstance.

The ten years Mr Green had already spent in the Colony had confirmed him in his opinions and attitudes. He came from a family of small gentry in the Midlands of England. When he left school his father purchased him a commission in a good cavalry regiment. Then in some financial disaster concerned with railway construction his father lost his money and young

Green, a lieutenant of two or three years standing, found he had no longer the income to maintain himself in a good cavalry regiment. So he resigned his commission and went off to the colonies of Australia. In New South Wales, thanks to an introduction to Government House, he was given a position in the Lands Department, and was sent across the Blue Mountains to adjudicate on the boundaries of sheep runs. There he married the handsome daughter of a gentleman settler and with her marriage settlement and his own cash and credit purchased a sheep run and achieved a certain affluence. Then the gold rush came and the quiet sleepy bush life was gone for ever. So the Colonial Secretary appointed Mr Green the Gold Commissioner and he had to spend his time riding through distant creeks and valleys trying to bring law and order to the rough chaos and to extract the licence fee from the diggers.

He was a stern man and dealt roughly with transgressors, sly grog dealers and people who would not or could not pay the licence fee.

As he rode over ridges and sidlings, through sandy creeks and eucalypt covered hills, he felt himself alike to some Roman proconsul in a distant and savage part of the Empire, bringing law and civilisation where it was not before. He rode a fine horse (his own, not some poor government nag) and was dressed in a well cut uniform with a sabre jangling by his side, two troopers trotting behind him. The diggers he looked upon with distrust and suspicion. Many were foreigners and Green possessed the England gentleman's sense of superiority, the feeling that he and his countrymen were better than these people who chattered in some incomprehensible lingo. And he knew that many of the foreigners were veterans of the European barricades, a potential danger to society. And the others were Irish, superstitious and seditious, people who hated England and the Queen and all that stood for. So Mr Green looked with his cold dark eyes at the groups of diggers splashing in the creek and felt that to some degree the very safety of the Colony might depend on how he dealt with these ruffians. He must keep them in a firm rein, yet not provoke an explosion, for the forces of order were weak, a few miserable troopers in whom Mr Green had little confidence.

*   *   *

In the Camp there were two assistant commissioners, a sub-commissioner, a clerk, a sergeant-major, a couple of sergeants and a dozen troopers. The sergeant-major, a big Irishman, was a fair enough fellow but who had sold himself to the master, as Pat said to the disapproval of the Major and Harry.

But the troopers, what a collection! The scum of Van Diemen's Land or hopeless Sydney paupers, people too lazy or incompetent to dig for gold. They were despised by the diggers in an open fashion while the police in turn hated the diggers. Perhaps the diggers, collectively, didn't really hate the troopers but just looked upon them as people beneath contempt. The hatred they kept for the Commissioner and his assistants who rode through the diggings in a semi-military fashion with troopers fawning at their heels like so many spaniel pups. The assistant commissioners were the cousins and poor relations of the gentry, educated young men without capital, and they had absolutely no knowledge of mining and certainly no sympathy with the diggers. And then they went around hunting for licences they looked as fierce as rat catchers' dogs and if a digger didn't have his licence his tent would be burned and his cradle smashed and he would be taken off to prison in irons and then hailed before a magistrate and fined five pounds. And even more these small-beer despots spoke to the diggers as if they were dogs.

"Ho, my man, where is your licence?" and so on.

So among the diggers there was a steady rumble of discontent, a sullen dislike for the Commissioner's Camp and all it contained and stood for. The discontent smouldered like a slow fire, waiting to catch on to something combustible to set a blaze going.

But enough of complaining! There was work to be done and gold to be found and perhaps a fortune to be won. So Barton and party set to work and shifted a mountain of dirt, but if their first claim was not a duffer it was almost so. They made an ounce or less a day, working like dogs, just enough to keep them going, scarcely wages. As they went deeper they had to timber the sides of the shaft to prevent the earth and gravel falling in, so two of the party went off to the bush to cut down trees and haul the trunks, the branches and the bark back to the claim. Every morning there was a foot or two of water in the hole, even though the river was running low, and it had to be bailed out.

The claim was worked this way: one man worked below digging out the dirt with a helper who filled the buckets while a third hauled them to the surface and carry the dirt to the cradle, where a fourth would do the washing and rocking. Even for George and Pat, accustomed as they were to labour, it was hard work. But to the two new chums, not used to this sort of thing, the first weeks digging from dawn to dusk was absolute agony, with stiff aching muscles and blistered hands. But somehow the example of their two mates led them to stick to the job. George was a little sorry for them, for they were rather like lost sheep strayed from the flock. After a month when their hands were properly calloused and their muscles hardened, then they could swing a pick with the best of them, and they had almost become different men.

It took George some time to find out why they had come to the Colony. In fact he never did find out, for their answers were a bit evasive. The Major, it seemed, was once an officer in a cavalry regiment in England and there must have been some trouble probably over gambling, thought George. Certainly in his spare time the Major loved to head and tail 'em and on Saturday nights he was always good for a game. And he didn't like to talk too much about his past, so George concluded that he might have good reason. There was one thing about the Major; he did know a thing or two about horses but with Harry Pole it was another matter. He was a pleasant enough companion, honest as far as anyone knew and who worked as well as he could. But there seemed a lack of determination, of the will to survive. Amelia would like him, thought George. He'd hand around the tea cups and sing when she played the piano. But send him out in the bush mustering cattle and sooner or later you would find him sitting under a tree completely lost

At night when they had eaten and were sitting by the fire drinking their way through a bottle of rum George would look at his companions and think: here are two fellows with the best of education (for Pole had fagged at Eton and been plucked at Oxford and the Major something similar) and brought up to consider themselves among the rulers. But compared to me and Pat, he thought, they are mere children. In the bush they are quite lost. They look to us for everything, we are in charge, we decide what shall be done. However, George shrugged his shoulders in his nonchalant way. Such was life. But he felt at heart that really, in truth, it was hard work that made men, not the mamby-pamby existence of the drawing room and the tea party; this was only for people who lived on the money their fathers accumulated. There was something about the life on the Turon that made George contemplative. When he awoke in the morning at first light he would go outside the tent and watch the sun come up over the dark hills to the east and listen to the awakening birds and watch the magpies that hopped around the tent waiting for scraps. Up and down the river people sleepily came out of their tents and fires were lit and smoke drifted in the gentle dawn wind, and gradually the deep valley and its nooks and crannies, from Bushrangers' Creek to Scabby Hill, from Heaths Point to Golden Gully, were lit by the sun.

It was good to be alive, thought George, alive and to work honestly and earn one's living as a free man, bound to no one, with good mates, enough to eat and drink, and there you were.

A couple of months on the Turon taught George a lot about gold and how to find it. He knew the difference between gold and fool's gold, he could work a pan quickly and well and was a good hand with the cradle. But the claim was still not going well. They bottomed on a hard cementy stuff, hard as stone and they thought they were down to bedrock. Tons of earth they put through the cradle. Yet despite all this back breaking work they were scarcely making tucker. Should they go on with the claim or look elsewhere? What to do? Let's ask someone who knows more than we do, said Pat. So they looked around.

A hundred yards upstream was a party working a claim. They were Cornish, stocky little men with chests like barrels and fists like legs of mutton. In a quiet sort of way they were friendly enough and if you asked them how things were going they would answer: "Oh, so-so." From the way they spoke they might just be making wages. The leader was a man named Henry Treganza. He was a little older than his mates and had a beard on his chin like a goat. At night when they sat around the fire he led in the singing of Methodist hymns. In Cornwall after the abolition of the import duty on foreign ore in 1845 many mines closed and miners were out of work and left Cornwall mostly for the United States. But Treganza for some reason chose New South Wales as his destination and in Sydney learned that copper was discovered near Bathurst and the owners of the mine were seeking experienced miners. He and three others went to Summerhill and not only mined copper but smelted it as well. A dray loaded with bright copper ingots occasionally went to Bathurst to show how profitable the operation was.

The miners had disputes with the owners now and then, who would threaten them with the Master and Servant Act. But still life was better than in Cornwall. Treganza often used to think what stupid and short sighted people the rulers of England were. They allowed their most skilled and useful subjects to be ill-treated at home and then sent to the ends of the earth, never to return. Indeed a bush humpy and a diet of unlimited mutton and damper made a better life than working in the deep, dank and dangerous dust filled tin mines of Cornwall, living in a tiny cottage that let in the rain, eating pilchards and potatoes until you died. Then the Turon Rush began and Treganza and his mates to the fury of the owners abandoned Summerhill and went off in search of gold. Because their age old practical experience of mining the Cornish always selected the best areas in which to stake their claims. Since 1851 they worked several claims and were said to have done well although they would never admit it.

So it was natural that George should go to Treganza for advice.

"You're thinkin' you're on bedrock, boay," said the Cornishman. "But it's only a false bottom. Under it's a gutter that runs a couple o' feet thick and pays an ounce to the barrer. Drive nor' and south but set the drive below the gutter so's the wash dirt's on the back."

"What back?" said George, not comprehending.

"Why, the top of the drive, of course."

Treganza scratched his beard.

"The cradle'll be a bit slow to treat the dirt, so's you'll better put in a long tom. The weather may change any time after Christmas and when the river flows high, then it's goodbye to river claims for weeks."

So George thanked the man for his advice and went into Sofala and purchased some black powder and a length of Bickford safety fuse. Then he and Harry Pole drove some holes into the false bottom and blasted through to the golden gulley that lay underneath.

*   *   *

Every Saturday night it was the custom of the diggers to go and enjoy themselves. On that day work ended about three in the afternoon and from then on until sunset it was the diggers' habit to tidy up their camps wash clothes, shave and trim their beards and hair and, if they could write, write letters to their homes and families -- that is if they had any.

So in fresh moleskins, red shirts, blue neckchiefs, stout boots freshly blackened, and cabbage tree hats they would stroll in groups through the short Australian twilight towards Sofala. As the hot sun sank over the dark and sinister mountains to the west all along the river the camp fires were lit and smoke drifted skyward and it was a charming and picturesque scene that met the eye. The diggers reckoned it was pretty safe to leave the claims and the tents; the Turon diggers were honest enough, and stay at home neighbours would keep an eye on things. Even during the day tents were left unattended while their owners worked and at night you could leave tools on the claim without risk of them being taken.

The diggers who walked towards the bright lights of the township were men who had all the week toiled hard, end-lessly .digging in the river gravel, endlessly shaking the cradles, endlessly washing dirt in the long toms and at the end of the day cleaning up by candle light to find how much gold, if any, was caught in the riffles. They wanted drink to stimulate their tired bodies, food to eat which they had not cooked themselves, the excitement of playing cards or toss halfpenny. When George and his mates reached the main street of Sofala it was as light as day. Hotels, theatres, the circus, all had their lights glaring. The shops were all open, displaying goods for the diggers' needs;

shovels, crowbars, hoppers, pannikins, tin dishes, tents, ropes, blocks, sledgehammers, wedges, pumps, dogskin bags for gold, revolvers, guns, axes and so forth.

Then there were the lemonade sellers shouting their wares, the haircutters, tailors, toothdrawers, bakers and butchers, all open for business until late at night.

First of all George and his friends decided they needed a meal. What better place than the Prospectors Hotel! Here was a great room with many tables crowded with people, with a band and girls who came from who knows where who danced with the great hairy diggers. Then dinner appeared; four great steaming plates of soup, then four great plates heaped with meat and vegetable, and a great plum duff to follow. Just the tucker for people come from working all week like slaves. They drank great pots of Colonial beer and finished with pots of steaming .black tea, laced with rum from the flask carried in Harry's pocket.

What next? What about Mr Ashley's circus? So they pushed their way through the crowd and took four tickets for the circus, which had just begun. Oh, it was funny and exciting to see the girls on horseback jumping through the hoops. And then a girl, a beautiful girl thought George, he'd never seen a more beautiful one, came into the centre of the ring and sang:

Oh, the blooming heather and the pale blue bell
In my bonnet then I wore;
And memory knows no brighter theme
Than those happy days or yore.
Scotland! Land of chief and song!
Oh, what charms to thee belong!

Then the crowd went mad and the Scots who were numerous among the diggers and often the most hardworking and successful threw their hats in the air and cheered and cheered.

At last, exhausted, they went out into the cool night air, and then Harry and the Major went off saying they were going to a game of toss halfpenny, so George and Pat went back to the Prospectors' Arms to have more tea topped up with rum, and drank and talked about the wonderful evening and the wonderful girl on the horse.

By now it was late and they decided it was time to go home. They left the crowded streets behind them and walked through the calm moonlight and finally came to the top of Ration Hill where they paused for breath. In the bright moonlight, almost as bright as day, the river flats stood out clear and the shadows were as black as ink.

George paused and stopped Pat in something he was saying. He could hear a noise, a little whimpering noise. He strode over to the shadow of a bush and peered into it.

"What's youse doin' there?" he asked.

"I'm not doin' no harm, mister," came the reply and out of the bushes came a girl, a thin slovenly girl of about fourteen or fifteen.

"Why, it's Eliza, who works at the Pick and Shovel!"

She nodded, sniffing.

"What are you doing here?"

"Well," said the girl, "I dropped a plate of soup in the dining room and the missus gave me a clip on the ear and called me a lazy Irish orphan bastard. So I picked up the plate and threw it at her, and then I run away."

"Have you got anywhere to go?" asked Pat.

"No, nowhere."

"Well, we can't leave you out in the bush all night, so you'd better come along with us, hadn't she, George?"

"Why, yes. We'll give her a blanket and she can sleep at the back of the tent."

"Come on, then."

So the girl limped out of the bushes and followed them down the track.

CHAPTER 6

The sub-assistant commissioner at Sofala was a Scot, Donald Maclean. He was a man of nearly forty, of medium height, strongly built, with a firm, well moulded face and greying hair and moustache. He was in the Colony for nigh on twenty years. His father was a small laird in Perthshire who owned a couple or three farms and a few acres he farmed himself. The parents saw to it that the children were well educated, even the girls, at a Blairgowrie school. When the boys reached manhood something needed to be done for them, some sort of billet found for each.

True the elder had the property, such as it was, but for the others they had to fend for themselves. The girls, of course, got married. One married a clergyman and another a writer to the signet and lived in Edinburgh, another an officer in a Highland regiment and the fourth a doctor who went to New Zealand.

As for the boys, one joined the East India Company's Bengal Infantry and was killed in some obscure skirmish, two purchased commissions in English regiments and the fourth joined the Excise but gave it up and went to Canada. And Donald found his way to Australia - the family, in truth, was scattered to the ends of the earth. Donald arrived in the Colony not long after the departure of Governor Darling, in the days when the System was still in operation. He came because a cousin of his father was an assistant in the commissary department and felt that a billet could be found for Donald in the Government service.

Donald, in fact, soon found a position with the auditor general's department and for fifteen years worked in a decrepit building in Bent Street, adding up figures all day and frequenting Dr Lang's Scots kirk on the opposite hill on Sundays. Through the long dreary voyage to the Colony, looking out on the vast grey expanse of the ocean, Donald thought longingly of his home, his family and the familiar lochs and forests of his native land. Why did Scots leave their homeland, he thought, and travel to the ends of the earth? Why did the compatriots of Burns and Scott migrate to far distant places by the thousand? Not only the dispossessed cotters, the dispossessed peasants of Sutherland and elsewhere, but educated people, too, people who could have made some substantial contribution to the life of their country. Donald thought, like Burns, that to migrate was in some way to betray his country; but what was the alternative except to live in grinding poverty, not to realise one's ambitions and potentials?

As the years passed and he became part of the Scottish community in Sydney the feeling of loss subsided and he adapted himself to the new country. But a letter from home, a chance meeting with a new arrival, even a picture in a book would bring back the old ache. He married the daughter of a fellow Scot but she died in childbirth. He found no further desire for domesticity and the occasional pricks of the flesh were satisfied haphazardly.

One day he found there was a vacancy for an assistant to the Commissioner for Lands in the Western District. He applied for the position and obtained it. He was delighted. This meant advancement, more money, a better life. During his time in the Colony he had never been further west than Parramatta. Now he took the Western Road, a flattering name for a rough bush track over the Blue Mountains to Bathurst. He found the work to be light, his senior, Mr Green, was often away settling problems of disputed boundaries farther out, or looking after his own estate. Donald found the climate, if warm in summer was to say the least bracing in winter and far superior to the muggy and enervating heat of the littoral. There was something about the place, something that he couldn't quite put a finger on, that pleased him. Perhaps it was because Sydney reminded him of a second class English provincial town, but when he walked up to the hill behind Bathurst and looked over the wide yellow-green plains that swept to the distant purple horizon he felt that here was something new, something different, beautiful and peaceful.

He soon made friends, for there were many Scots settlers in the district. He had comfortable lodgings and enough work to keep him busy. Then that fat fool Hargraves revealed that there was gold near Bathurst and the whole place went mad. The Colony was turned upside down. Great crowds of people came streaming up the Western Road, some in coaches others in carts and drays, others on horseback, many on foot. He once saw a man wheeling a barrow followed by his wife and children, bound for the goldfields! The Government in Sydney put Mr Green in charge of the goldfields. This was in 1651, when all was new. And in a few months not only Ophir was filled with diggers, but Sofala, previously an unknown crossing over the river, became a town overnight.

And the diggers like an advancing army, pressed on to the Meroo and Louisa Creek, down south to Tuena and westward to unknown creeks and flats where little settlements sprang up in a few days, to last for months or years, according to the luck of the field. So what was previously a quiet backwater where gentlemen settlers ruled over sheep and untold acres became a centre of excitement, filled with thousands of turbulent people. And how the gentleman settlers hated the change! Hitherto everything was their way, with an ever rising price for wool and labour in the form of people who had no alternative but to work as shepherds or hut keepers. At Bathurst, a long settled area, there was now a new generation of settlers, people born in the Colony or who had come there as children and had really never known any other life. The older settlers were gradually going to their reward in the hereafter.

Colonel Duncan died not long before the discovery of gold, Captain Piper soon after and Major Morisset and Captain Sutherland were very old and shaky. The generation of Waterloo and the Peninsula were gradually fading away. Colonel Duncan's son, Jamie, became a particular friend of Donald. Jamie inherited a fine property not far from the town and in a big red brick house he lived with his wife, his mother and an unmarried sister. The mother, much younger than the old Colonel, was a stiff, proud woman, but devoted to her son. Jamie was married to a quiet little woman, the daughter of a Scottish settler on the Hunter, and she gave birth to a child every year. There were five already and indications that another was to be expected. Jamie's mother had her own rooms in the house and lived separately from the others with her own servant.

The elder daughter, Elizabeth, was married to a Presbyterian clergyman who lived in Sydney. The younger, Maria, was unmarried, about thirty years of age and lived at home. She had sandy blond hair that always got in her eyes and she kept herself busy looking after the chickens and ducks, the vegetable garden and the orchard. Donald was a frequent visitor to the Duncan home. Jamie, who left Scotland as a child, would ask Donald all sorts of questions about the place and talk with nostalgia of one day going back. Mrs Duncan made it evident to Donald that he was welcome in the house. No doubt she wished to find a husband for her remaining daughter; it was an embarrassment to have the big raw boned thirty year old girl around the house, a girl who should years ago have been bedded down with a man.

One day Mr Green informed Donald that he had to go to the Turon as sub commissioner, a post that carried with it the pleasant enough salary of two hundred pounds a year. So one afternoon he rode over to the Duncan place to say goodbye. He had a nice horse, his equipment was well kept and he wore a smart, semi-military uniform. When he arrived he found Jamie was away in a distant paddock and Mrs Duncan was upstairs. Maria received him with admiring glances. Donald looked keenly at her; her eyes were shining, her cheeks were pink and she brushed a rather attractive strand of hair from her cheek. He was drawn to her. And now he was off to the barbarous Turon where he would be stationed for heavens knows how long.

He knew she liked him, she was a well-shaped girl for all -her awkwardness and would surely improve with marriage. In fact a good Scots lass even if a little raw in her movements and she had a high somewhat freckled completion which the dry climate of the Australian inland did not treat kindly. Jamie was sandy haired too, shortish, stocky and always busy from morn to night on his property. In his father's time, in the days of transportation, there were plenty of assigned servants around the house but now, apart from two or three Highlanders who could scarcely speak English and who had been with the family for years, there was no labour to be had. Jamie kept cattle and a few horses. The estate contained some good river land which he had let out to small farmers who cultivated vegetables. The amount these people earned was disgraceful, Mrs Duncan would say with great indignation. They would take a dray load of cabbages to the Turon and sell them for a shilling each! Despite the rage of the big landowners the gold rush brought prosperity to many. The thousands of hungry diggers needed a multitude of goods and were ready to pay high prices. The country shopkeepers, the hotel keepers, anyone with cattle and sheep for sale, were sure of good profits. And there was the surprising rise in the price of everything, including land.

It was quiet in the Duncan drawing room and dark, too, for the curtains were drawn against the sunlight glare.

"I've come to say goodbye, Miss Duncan," said Donald. "I've been ordered to the Turon and I'm likely to be away for some time. True, it's only thirty miles from here, but my duties will keep me busy, I'm feared."

She came quite close to him and said she was sorry he was leaving. Suddenly, almost without knowing why, they were in each other's arms, and she kissed him most passionately, while his hands clasped her to him.

"Oh, Maria," he gasped. "I love you."

They stood breathless. There were sounds outside and they stepped apart. Mrs Duncan came into the room and Donald stammered his goodbyes to both the women.

"I must see Jamie before I go," he said.

Jamie he found riding back to the house. When he learned that Donald wanted to marry his sister he was most pleased.

"I couldn't ask for anyone better," he said. "That fellow Browne who lives at Five Creeks has been paying attention to her. He's English and an Episcopalian and I can scarcely bear to be polite to him. I'd hate to have him for a brother in law.

*   *   *

It was understood that the question of marriage would be put off until Donald could find a more settled position. He might become an assistant commissioner in time or find some other billet in the public service which would enable him to maintain Maria in the way she was accustomed. Mrs Duncan was quietly satisfied and Maria was content with the thought of abandoning her spinsterhood for a good husband, for there was no doubt that Donald was an excellent and steady fellow. So off he went to the Turon in his fine uniform with the silver braid, with a trooper at his back and a spare horse to carry his kit. Common diggers and others on the Turon track gave him hostile looks as he passed by.

At Sofala he was billeted at the Camp, sited on the other side of the river from the town. His duties were mainly in the office taking licence fees, keeping records, attending to the troopers' pay and all the dull administrative details of the place. Mr Green's office was in Bathurst for he was commissioner for all the Western goldfields which covered a large area. But Sofala was the centre of the biggest conglomeration of diggers and possessed two assistant commissioners in addition to Donald. The senior of the two was William Percival Drake, a young man in his late twenties. Before he joined the commission he was a clerk of the court at Goulburn. His uncle came to the Colony in the time of Governor Darling and took up a big grant of land on the Monaro where he ran many thousands of sheep on the windswept plains. The uncle used his influence at Government House to find the nephew a position suitable to his station. Drake who came to the Colony before the gold rush, was impeccable in his dress and liked to parade his troopers and inspect their accoutrement. This was a hard task indeed, for the troopers were a sad and useless lot, as all agreed. It was really a waste of time for Drake to chivvied them, make them polish their boots, saddle soap their horse furniture, oil their carbines and keep their sabres sharp.

The commissioners messed together in a tent and Drake, who had at one time been in the army, insisted on military etiquette and the three of them always toasted the Queen before they opened their cigar cases.

The other assistant commissioner was new to the Colony. He came from Ireland, although it would be hard to call him an Irishman. He was a nephew of the Earl of Sligo and his name was Arthur Waterford. The previous year he arrived in the Colony with the inevitable letter of introduction to the Governor. He too had been in army but why he left a good cavalry regiment to come to New South Wales he never cared to say. He was a gay enough fellow and mad about horses and his main complaint about the Colony was that it had no foxes and no hedges. He often talked about how foxes should be introduced and rabbits, too, for shooting. Donald's opinion was that Drake was as shallow as a piece of paper and had not an idea in his head, a not unfrequent characteristic of the Saxon. But Drake and Waterford had much in common. It was evident to Donald that they put him in a different category to themselves. True enough he was technically classed as a gentleman but he spoke with a Scottish burr and he was some sort of a Presbyterian, which was better than being a Dissenter but not quite the same as being a member of the Established Church.

Another difference between them and Donald was that he conversed freely with diggers. It is true that they were usually the Scots diggers and Donald was only too happy to converse man to man with his compatriots. But talk to diggers! These were people one did not talk to. You might give them orders, tell them to produce a licence or you might decide what was right and what was wrong in some dispute over a claim — but to converse with them as if they were your equals, that was most strange, according to the views of the other commissioners.

Now and then Mr Green with his grim visage and hard eyes came to the Turon on a tour of inspection. He had an inquiring mind and asked many questions of an intelligent nature which to Donald, who knew the man well, indicated that he recognised some of the realities of the situation.

The one or two sergeants and the dozen or so troopers in the Camp were ruled over by Sergeant-Major Dogherty, a great upstanding Irishman, a real Irishman with a brogue you could cut with a knife. Dogherty was an ex-sergeant of cavalry and knew his soldiering. If he ran the troopers with a light hand it was because he knew they were poor material and there was not much to do with them except to see that they were reasonably neat and didn't get drunk or steal more than could be helped. Fundamentally Dogherty had a strong sense of natural justice and while he strictly administered the law he combined his administration with a certain amount of common sense. He was therefore not unpopular with the diggers and he was active in the pursuit of the bushrangers and robbers who battened on the goldfields. So the diggers thought he was a good man, even if he was a policeman.

As Donald was aware there was much unrest on the diggings. He felt the regulations were unjust, but this was the law and he was therefore obliged by his position to see that it was administered. No doubt it would be changed in time but until then the law had to be observed. Such was the way he thought.

There were associations of diggers set up and petitions and memoranda sent to the Legislative Council in Sydney. Not only the diggers wanted the regulations changed but also the people who ran the quartz mining companies and the big syndicates that employed wages men. And the shopkeepers were resentful, too, for they had to pay the licence fee. In fact anyone on the goldfields had to pay, and that included clergymen and school-teachers and doctors.

Some were more resentful than others and these were mainly the diggers who worked in small parties. Among them were those who were prepared to place a ban on the payment of the licence and let the troopers try to arrest them, which would inevitably result in a violent collision. Others were moral force people, and there were others who simply couldn't be bothered and so went off to the Victorian diggings where rich fields were continually being discovered. So there was a small but steady stream of diggers who turned their backs on the troubled Turon and took the track to the Ovens River, Ballarat or Bendigo.

Donald found one of his duties was to visit now and then the major publicans and storekeepers in the town, to find their opinions of the unrest and perhaps the names of those most active in the digger associations. The publicans in particular were dependent on the goodwill of the commissioners for their licence and were always ready to talk. Then there were two or three men who slipped into the Camp after dark and held discreet conversations with Sergeant-Major Dogherty. So at the Camp a picture was built up of who was on the field, who the trouble-makers were, who sided with the government and what the generality of diggers thought.

This was important, Mr Green told Donald in a moment of confidence, for the situation was slowly developing towards a confrontation between the two sides. Sooner or later there would be a crisis, he said, and the more that was known about the diggers' movement the better one would be able to deal with it.

CHAPTER 7

John Murdoch was the junior partner in McFee and Company, merchants, whose warehouse was in Kent Street overlooking Darling Harbour. Murdoch's father was a linen manufacturer in Belfast, a staunch Protestant and Orangeman. But the son, towards his twenty second year, developed a weakness in the chest and the Belfast doctors warned him that he should seek a milder climate for the sake of his health. Of his eight brothers and sisters, two brothers and one of the girls were already dead of an inflammation of the lungs. Off he was sent to New South Wales and he arrived in the Colony about a year before the discovery of gold. He came with an introduction to Mr McFee who was his father's cousin and he was given a minor clerking position in the company. But John Murdoch was a meticulous and careful young man with an eye for detail. He did his job well and soon obtained advancement. Then came the gold rush and half the clerks in the company went off to Ophir and as well there was a big demand for goods and twice as much work as before. By the time the gold rush was in its second year Murdoch was so important to the company that he was offered and accepted a junior partnership. Despite the amount of work he did, his health improved in the good Sydney sunshine and he felt better and with more energy than before.

Mr McFee owned a fine house at Glebe. It was brand, spanking new, the product of handsome Colonial profits, full of new furniture from England, in the latest style. It stood in its own grounds with a stable at the rear which housed a groom and a four-wheeler and a horse, which took Mr McFee off to his office every morning and brought him back at six in the evening, clip-clop, in a stately and refined manner. Mr and Mrs McFee frequently entertained — not the .stuck up Anglicans and dissolute Government House lot — respectable merchants and their families, mostly of the Methodist persuasion.

There were three McFee daughters, all very nubile and eager to talk to young Murdoch, and a pimply adolescent son of about sixteen who according to Mr McFee was difficult to deal with. Being with Mr McFee all day at the office and frequently at the house in the evening Murdoch felt himself inexorably drawn into the family. The elder daughter all smiles and budding breasts seemed inevitably seated next to him. He was at first attracted to her but suddenly began to feel that a trap was being set for him. On Saturday afternoons Murdoch liked nothing better than to slip down to Sydney Cove to hire a boat and row around the point to Garden Island. And on Sunday mornings after chapel he would hire a horse and go sometimes as far as South Head. He would return invigorated and the glorious climate seemed to fill him with new energy and a sort of well-being.

He had a few friends, mainly young men of his own age engaged in commerce or banking or assurance. Once or twice a month three or four of them would meet for dinner at the Metropolitan Hotel in Pitt Street or if they wanted to be really daring at the Cafe Restaurant Francais in George Street, near Margaret Street. They met one evening in autumn and one of the party brought with him a client, a jovial man who owned a big sheep station near Goulburn. After dinner, which was ample and include wine, the party in a happy mood lay back in the chairs and puffed pipes.

"Well, lads," said Mr Forrest, the Goulburn squatter, "What shall we do now?"

They all looked at him, curious.

"What about a visit to Madam Rose?"

"Madam Rose?" asked Murdoch. "Who's she?"

"You must know Madam Rose!" said Dick Tanner, who worked at the Union Bank. Murdoch didn't but began to have the suspicion that this might not be an outing best to mention to Mr McFee.

So they left the restaurant and strolled through the town to a quiet and discreet house in College Street where Mr Forest knocked on the door and they were let in by a maid to an elaborately furnished reception room. Madam Rose entered and welcomed Mr Forrest as an old friend.

"Want to see the girls, gentlemen?" she asked and soon several young women, plump and amiable, full of smiles and little jokes, came into the room. Wine was served and after a few minutes of chitchat Mr Forrest disappeared upstairs. Murdoch's two companions laughed heartily and themselves went off with the two other girls. There was only one left, sitting beside Murdoch. She was a pale slip of a thing, pert, with red lips and a piquant expression.

"Finish your drink, John," she said, "and we'll go upstairs for a while."

Murdoch's mind was in a state of turmoil. He was in a house of sin and his eternal soul might be damned for ever, condemned to everlasting hell fire. If he was to give way to sin he would be rejecting Jesus who died for his sake. He said all this to himself but it did not sound quite rational. But he had often suffered the pricks of the flesh and for years was tormented by sinful thoughts. And the good meal he had just eaten, the pleasant wine he had just drunk, the gay company, the relaxed atmosphere, all helped to weaken his resolve. But he trembled; how could he face Mr McFee and his daughters, his friends among the Methodist clergy if he committed sinful fornication. But at that moment, just as he prevaricated, there came a knock on the door. He heard a voice he knew — Brown of Boorawa — a wealthy squatter, a frequent visitor to the McFee household when he was in Sydney.

"Is Mary in?" he heard him ask.

"No, Mr Brown," answered Madam Rose. "she's busy at the moment, but little Annie would be glad to see you, I'm sure."

The thought of being caught in the house by Mr Brown was too much for Murdoch. He took the girl's hand and they slipped through a door at the back of the room. They stood in a dark passageway. his heart was beating fast. The girl pressed herself against him; she smelt strongly of cheap and pungent perfume that tickled his nostril in a provocative manner.

"Come to my room, Johhnie dear," she whispered, taking him by the hand. And he followed obediently.

*　　*　　*

Sydney was in the grip of a terrible excitement. Every day new ships appeared in Port Jackson and masses of people crowded ashore. Some were honest migrants, other paupers shovelled out on ships and sent to the Colony to be rid of, and other ships arrived filled with Irish orphan girls, wretched children whose parents died in the famine and were dispatched to the Colony in the hope that they would become wives of bushmen or servants to the gentry.

These strange lost people wandered about the streets mingling with the old Sydneysiders, the respectable, the larrikin gangs from The Rocks, the sailors off passing ships, the diggers returned from the Turon, the redcoat garrison and the gentry who rode in carriages and who turned their nose up at the mob. For every digger who returned from the goldfields disconsolate there were a dozen men who wanted to go and try their luck up the country, who dreamed of the fortune to be picked up in some lonely creek.

There was work everywhere. New houses were being built, warehouses were needed for the goods flooding into the country, labour was scarce, wages were high, money was flowing in the hotels and eating houses. From the ships' holds there poured into the town every sort of produce: ladies bonnets, cases of claret and champagne, pick axes and shovels, men's clothing, furniture, crowbars, rum and a thousand other items. Every day in Sydney drays took off up the country carrying goods to far flung diggings, either south to Araluen, west to the Turon or to the new diggings opening up on the road to Moreton Bay.

And while the great landholders with their vast flocks of merinos looked gloomily at the terrible changes that were shaking the Colony, swearing that the country was ruined and would never be the same again due to the spread of democratic sentiments, the merchants thought differently They were doing great business as a result of the gold, building up important merchant houses, because their trade was doubled and tripled in two years, allowing them to accumulate considerable fortunes. It was true that the democratic sentiments of the diggers were a bit frightening but the Colony could not for ever be just a sheep farm; progress had to come whether the squatters liked it or not.

As a result of profiting from the situation Mr McFee and Murdoch were up to their ears in work. Mr McFee was feeling his age and more and more of the work fell on the shoulders of young Murdoch. This young man now began to feel that the McFee household was rather boring, that the McFee daughters were dull and pretentious young women. He began to look askance at Mrs McFee, wondering if she considered him to be a potential son-in-law — a thought that appalled him Now, no longer did he on Sunday frequent the Methodist Chapel for he preferred the bright Australian sunshine to the clergyman's gloomy prognostications of everlasting damnation for sinners and the dreary hymns sung by the grim self-satisfied congregation.

He sought company further afield. His commercial friends were really a bit dull. Being naturally inclined to the liberal point of view rather than to the crusty old conservatism of the wool barons he took to frequenting the company of young Henry Parkes, the editor of The Empire newspaper, voice of the liberals and radicals, and who hoped to enter the Legislative Council after the next election. At Parkes' home he met the brilliant young Dan Deniehy, an Australian native, the poet Harpur and a young journalist named David Blair. Harpur and Deniehy seemed proud of their native birth, as if to be born Australian put them above the migrant. Parkes was eloquent and indignant about the way the Colony was run.

"The Governor," he said, "Sir Charles Augustus FitzRoy, is a weak debauchee, a gambler, who can't manage his own affairs, let alone those of the Colony and leaves the reins of power in the hands of the Colonial Secretary, Deas Thomson, who is the real ruler of the Colony and who rules in the interests of the big settlers. Not long ago the Governor got in the family way the daughter of a publican and he had to pay her father two hundred pounds to keep the scandal quiet."

Henry Parkes, who was about thirty years old, was the man who spoke most passionately at the great meeting held in 1849 at Circular Quay in the midst of a downpour of rain to protest against the landing of convicts from the vessel *Hashemy*, and which resulted finally in the ending of the transportation system.

His fervour sometimes frightened John Murdoch, for Parkes wanted all sorts of radical and revolutionary things, such as universal suffrage, payment of members of parliament and the ballot, and he even hinted at the independence of the Colony from British rule.

Dan Deniehy frankly admitted to being a republican and once confessed to Murdoch that he thought Parkes was not sincerely of this opinion.

"There's too much Englishism about Parkes," he said. "One day he'll sell out the cause of the Australian republic."

It was their custom to meet in a little parlour behind Parkes' shop in Hunter Street where he sold all sorts of articles made from ivory. Deniehy was a strange and brilliant little fellow, thought Murdoch, and his parents, it seems, like those of the poet Harpurh were convicts. He was only about five feet high, with a cadaverous yellow, freckled face, brilliant eyes and a shock of tow-coloured hair. He was a brilliant talker, one of the most intellectual conversationalists in the Colony. However, despite the differences of opinion, they were all united in hatred of the great gentleman settler, Wentworth, whose plan for a new constitution was a conspiracy against the rights of the people and which would hand over millions of square miles of land to the woolly lords who would run sheep on it, aided by their servants, ill paid wretches or semi-slave coolies.

Usually about once a week, always after dark, Murdoch would slip over to College Street and knock on Madam Rose's door and ask for Alice, for that was the name of the girl who first led him from the path of righteousness. She always made him welcome, as if she was really glad to see him. One evening he knocked at the door and Madam Rose told him Alice was busy.

"But there's Annie or Mary or Margy who'll all be glad to see you," she said.

He thanked Madam Rose and went away, strangely upset. He thought of Alice in the arms of some hairy sea captain or a rough squatter from the outback down in Sydney on the spree. He remembered how in recent time she always seemed so happy to see him, so affectionate in her embraces. He felt strangely lonely without her. She gave him confidence when he was with her, as well as physical comfort. Business kept him busy for the next few days, for a number of men of affairs in Sydney were interested in gold mining in a more scientific manner and were considering the formation of a company to mine reef gold. The government, when approached, indicated that it would be prepared to grant larger tracts of land to such companies, rather than small areas to individual diggers. Mr McFee intended to take up a considerable holding in the company and John Murdoch was to have a seat on the board of management to make sure the money was wisely spent.

But he found it hard to keep thoughts of Alice out of his mind. Her company gave him a sort of mental calm. Something of her history she had confided to him and he knew she was worried about the fate of her sister who had run away from Madam Rose and was supposed to have gone to the goldfields. Murdoch found he was now supposed to travel to the Turon to visit the site of the proposed mine. The company employed a mining expert, a Mr Tregoning, who was prepared to show the directors the area he had selected. So Murdoch and a Mr Bowden, representing other capital interests, would go together to inspect the area and learn something of the work.

This meant an absence of over a week, even two or three, from Sydney. A few days before the date of his departure Murdoch left his office on a pretext and walked across the park to College Street. Yes, Alice was free, said Madam Rose, aroused from her afternoon nap and amused by Murdoch's eagerness. Alice embraced him passionately. "I've got to go up the country," Murdoch told her. "And I couldn't go without seeing you."

They lay exhausted on the bed, with the sunlight filtering through the lace curtains that Madam Rose insisted should be on every window to give an impression of respectability. Sud-

THE PLACE OF GOLD

denly Alice burst into tears.

"Oh, Johnnie," she cried. "I love you so. I don't want any man but you!"

He buried his face in her warm, soft shoulder.

"Alice, Alice," he said. "I love you, too."

Now it was time to go and she clung to him weeping. What to do? He must take her away from College Street, but where to? She could not come to his lodgings. So he made a quick decision in the way he was accustomed to in business, and which had brought him such rapid promotion in Mr McFee's house. He told her he would be back that evening to take her away.

"But Madam Rose won't let me go. She says I owe her money. She'll get Bill the Basher to stop me!"

"No matter," said Murdoch decisively. "Have some things wrapped in a bundle. It'll be all right."

With that he dressed quickly, told her he would be back later and went to his office. At six he hurried out again and went to look for lodgings. In a small house in Goulburn Street he found two little rooms to let on the first floor. He told the landlord they were for a young lady, his cousin, not long arrived in the Colony. He paid a month's rent and the red faced landlord, who smelt of rum, took the money with a smile.

Then Murdoch walked rapidly back to College Street, brushed past the servant who opened the door and ran upstairs to Alice's room. She was waiting for him, dressed for the street, with a few belongings done up in a bundle. As they went down the stairs Madam Rose came out of the kitchen, Bill the Basher behind her.

"What's this Alice?" she cried. "You can't leave here. You owe me money still."

"I owe you nothing, you old bitch!" cried Alice and before either Madam Rose or Bill the Basher could move she and her lover were out of the front door and away up the street.

CHAPTER 8

All four were gathered around the cradle; George, Pat, the Major and Harry Pole. Pat put a shovel of dirt into the hopper and the Major poured pots of river water on the heap. George rocked the cradle while Harry Pole removed the bigger stones by hand. This went on for five or ten minutes until the dirt was dissolved and ran out at the bottom. Finally George ceased rocking the contraption and then took out one of the two trays that fitted under the hopper. Into a pan placed on the ground he scraped the material caught in the riffles. He poked about with blunt fingers. Among the grains were specks of fine gold and some coarse, waterworn nuggets. Then he straightened himself.

"We're on it, lads! A golden hole!"

The other diggers at Green Point looked up as they heard the cheers and saw hats fly in the air.

"There's about half a pennyweight to a dish," said George.

They all made rapid mental calculations.

"At sixty buckets to the load that makes three ounces to the load, or about eleven pounds worth," said Pat. For all his illiteracy, he could calculate better than most.

"If we put in a long tom," said George, "we can put through two loads a day or even more."

"We'll be rich," said the Major, "if we can keep this up for a few weeks."

Then they set to work with great enthusiasm, inspired by the thought of the riches that lay beneath their feet. Harry and the Major worked in the hole while George and Pat, being practical bush carpenters, set to work to cut and haul timber for the long tom.

The river was still flowing well, so when they dug a race from the water's edge a little upstream to the long tom itself there was an ample flow. The long tom consisted of an open box about ten feet long into which the wash dirt was shovelled. The lighter material was washed into another open box with a plate to hold back the pebbles. The mixture of water and dirt then ran across timber riffles nailed to the bottom of the box, which caught the heavier particles. It was an effective enough operation and the four mates worked all the daylight hours to keep it supplied with washing stuff. Luckily for them there was little Eliza to look after the camp and prepare the meals, which meant more time for work, more time to extract the gold.

It was spring now and the weather on the Turon was delightful with warm days and fresh evenings. George and his friends, however, were too busy with the claim to notice the state of the weather. Every day after cleaning up they found four or even five or six ounces in the pan. At seventy shillings an ounce this meant sometimes twenty pounds a day, and their money belts grew fatter.

The shaft was now more than twenty feet deep into the ground and well driven through the cemented false bottom into the alluvial dirt that contained the gold. Now it was time to drive along the gulley in each direction and in view of the nature of the soil the drive had to be timbered. This meant that now and then two of the party went off into the bush to cut timber. Also the shaft was too deep for a whip and a windlass had to be constructed. There was a constant seepage at the bottom of the hole so a Californian pump was purchased. If the party's muscles were hard before, now they were like steel. If they worked long hours before, now they worked from dawn to dusk.

Every evening the result of the day's work was cleaned up. The tent opening was covered to keep out unwelcome visitors and they all sat around the rough table, the light of a flickering candle illuminating their bronzed faces. Placed in pannikins by the fire was the gold mixed with dirt taken that day from the riffles of the long tom or the cradle. One at a time the pannikins were placed on a sheet of white paper and the sand blow away. Then a magnet was passed over the heap to draw off any grains of iron stone. The impurities removed there lay upon the table the yellow glittering precious gold which could make a poor man rich, the equal of anyone, independent of the masters. even a master himself. People who had been insulted and humiliated, looked down upon and sneered at by the masters, who worked all day for a pittance or who rotted their lives away in some distant shepherd's hut, were now equal to anyone, and all because they possessed a dog skin bag full of gold.

The diggers now began to look anxiously at the sky. It was of a clear, delicate blue. The previous July there were thunderstorms that filled the river and washed out the bed claims for weeks. A flood now, when they were doing so well, would be disastrous. As Mr Treganz advised they dug well below the level of the gutter and began to drive downstream, timbering as they went. Although the river level was falling there was still enough water for the long tom. After a weekly visit to the gold buyer they would take the expenses out of the money, give Eliza a pound - more money than she had ever earned in her life before - and divide the remainder into four equal parts. Then every Saturday night after leaving Eliza to mind the camp they went off to Sofala to celebrate, to come home in the early hours of the morning, or sometimes not at all, for the Major and Harry usually went off to lose their hard earned money playing heads and tails. In the course of this they would drink rum until they could no longer walk and fall by the wayside to sleep under a bush, like so many other victims of the besotted inebriety so regularly found at the diggings and about which Mr Green complained bitterly in his reports to the Colonial Secretary.

*   *   *

As the year of 1852 drew to a close, there was a growing tense-
ness in the atmosphere on the Turon The diggers were uneasy,
indignant about the gold regulations, certain that the Government was hostile towards them. With angry eyes they watched
when the commissioners ventured out of the Camp on a licence
hunt.

"Joe, Joe!" The cry would echo along the flats. The young gentleman in his smart uniform with silver braid caracolling on a
good horse, followed by a servile hang-dog trooper, went past
with his nose in the air. And when he came to a digger working a
claim he would say:

"Ho, my good man, where is your licence?"

And the good man would scowl, spit on the ground and with
thick, calloused fingers would grope in his pockets and produce a dirty piece of paper which he would hand to the commissioner. The commissioner would look at it and without a
work of thanks give it back to the digger and ride off, as often
or not splashing the digger with mud from the horse's hooves.
And among themselves the diggers were indignant that they
paid taxes but had no representation. They paid thirty shillings
a month, however much gold they produced, enough to keep
a man in rations for three weeks and more than a gentleman
settler paid each year for a square mile of land. And they were
ruled over by ignorant boys who knew naught of mining, whose
salaries were paid from the licence fees and yet who hated and
despised the diggers who paid it, who looked down on them and
who could not even address them properly.

If a man was found without a licence he was taken to the log
lockup in handcuffs and next day fined by the magistrate, who
was also the commissioner. And if the commissioner was in a

bad humour or if the digger had offended him in some way, he'd tell the trooper to smash the man's cradle and set his tent on fire, which vile deeds he was entitled to do under the law. The diggers were certain that the arrogant popinjays could never work a claim with their lilywhite hands, scarcely knew the difference between a cradle and a long tom and had none of the practical qualities and skills needed to survive in the bush. So it became a matter of honour to deceive the commissioners. When one appeared on the field on a licence hunt the men with licences would scurry up a creek or into the bush and after a long chase by the commissioner and his trooper would stop and say in apparent surprise:

"What! Yer wanted ter see me licence, then? Why didn't yer say so?"

And he would meekly hand the licence to the sweating and angry commissioner who scarcely appreciated this form of plebeian humour. In the meantime those without licences had made themselves scarce.

What was the need for this semi-military force, said the diggers, except to persecute the diggers so they would be forced back to tailing sheep? The diggers were generally honest and they kept the field in order and any man caught stealing was likely to get a drubbing and be expelled from the area as George had once seen. But around about were gangs of bushrangers, usually ex-convicts from Van Diemens Land, who held up travellers and caused all sorts of violence and brutality. But this went on unhindered almost, for the police were usually too busy chasing and persecuting the diggers.

The high licence fee and the arrogance of the commissioners were not the only complaints. Why, traders in the field, doctors and even clergymen had to pay the licence fee. Too few inns were permitted and the sly grog shops did a roaring trade. Many were raided but some were carefully left alone, and people believed that the lucky ones escaped because they bribed the police. The revolt was beginning to take form. The Tambaroora diggers already had sent a well formulated petition to the Governor and the Sofala miners set up an association to protect their interests. Also, the diggers had friends in Sydney. Not among the Government House mob, to be sure, but in the shape of Mr Parkes and his newspaper, the Empire, which supported their cause. And if Mr Parkes to the Legislative Council, as they all hoped, then able to put the case for the diggers even more.

The diggers' other champion, the turbulent Dr John Dunncre Lang, regularly from his pulpit in the Scots Kirk in Sydney preached hell fire and damnation against the shepherd kings. He was the man who wanted freedom and independence for the golden lands of Australia! After his election to the Legislative Council he visited the Turon to preach to the diggers on the flat at Sofala. These rough men, usually so indifferent to religion, flocked in great numbers to hear him. The good doctor liked the diggers. He saw them as an instrument to achieve the independence of the country and the creation of an Australian republic, peopled by worthy and industrious small farmers, artisans and honest traders.

He said that taxation without representation was robbery and that the land was the gift of God to all and not to the few, and that the lands of Australia should be unlocked for honest and hardworking farmers. This met with a roar of approval for the diggers knew that sooner or later the gold would be mined out and they would have to seek other work. They wanted land so they could have a farm, a neat homestead by a creek, and bring up their families to a life of honest labour.

As the year wore on and the weather became really warm the air in the deep valley of the Turon was heavy and oppressive. With Christmas coming many diggers left the field to return home for the festival or, if they had no families, to dissipate their hard-earned wealth among the night lights of Bathurst or Sydney. The water level on the river slowly fell and it was a hard job for George's party to keep the long tom working. There was a plague of black snakes, the flies were worse than ever and fleas and mosquitoes abounded. There was sickness, too. Dysentery and Colonial fever and an outbreak of sandy blight. The hospital was full and there were frequent pathetic processions to the cemetery on the hill by the racecourse.

Both Harry Pole and the Major suggested that the party break up for Christmas. They were eager to spend on high living the money earned from the claim. But George took his example from the Cornish miners. They were working harder than ever.

"You'll see," said Henry Treganza. "If the weather changes as it often does at this time of year the river will flow a banker, as the Colonials say, and the bed claims will be under feet of water for weeks. Get out what you can while you can, I say."

So they laboured on, sunburnt and dusty, with muscles hardened, sometimes wet to the waist when they worked the long tom. Every evening after the meal they gathered in the tent like conspirators and, by the light of a lamp, cleaned up the gold obtained during the day and put it away in little dog skin bags.

*   *   *

When Eliza was brought to the camp she was rigged up a little slip tent at the back of the main tent where the men slept. Next morning Harry Pole and the Major appeared all bleary eyed and shaky and were mildly astonished. But George said:

"My word, she's a good little worker and I reckon she'll make a proper good cook for us."

So it was agreed that she should be put in charge of the catering. Every morning, then, she was up at dawn cooking chops for breakfast and then at midday would have a slice of damper and a bit of cold meat ready, and in the evening there would be a roast or a stew with potatoes or cabbage, if they were available. It was much better tucker than the diggers' were capable of preparing for themselves. And by the fire there was always a pot of black tea to drunk from pannikins with lots of sugar. Every day Eliza would walk over to the little village called Walberton about a mile away to buy meat and flour or tea, sugar and other rations.

In less than a week she was thoroughly at home. George she adored from the start. She realised that he was the acknowledged leader of the party by right of ability. He treated her kindly and with respect in the way bushmen treat women and she loved him for it. Pat she liked too. A good useful fellow and a good mate. The Major and Harry Pole were different. They were more like the men her sister used to go with in the Haymarket. Eliza sometimes felt sorry for the Major. He had fits of black depression that lasted for days. Most of his money went on gambling and every Saturday night he came back with his pockets empty. Harry Pole, his fair hair bleached by the sun, his once fresh complexion burned brown, was different again. The Major could look after himself, providing he was sober and hadn't lost all his money at cards or toss halfpenny, but Harry needed someone to tell him what to do. George would say:

"Look, Harry, take a shovel and a pick and work in the hole this morning."

So Harry would graft away quite effectively and honestly until he was told to do something else. The Major might have a worm burrowing in his brain, but not Harry.

Eliza found him pleasant enough, even amiable, but of no great profundity, a fellow who took life as it came. If he hadn't fallen .in with George he would be working for wages in some very humble capacity. Eliza often wondered why Harry and the Major ever came to Australia. They were not driven out by hard poverty as she and her sister were. Neither were they ambitious people who came to the Colony to make their way in farming or trade, It must have been, she thought, for some shameful reason. In England they would be gentlemen, would never work with their hands, never have to toil all day in the burning sun.

She was now long enough in the Colony to realise that it was a topsy-turvy sort of place. Most of the diggers were humble people but there was a London barrister in a party across the river who asserted that he made more money at the diggings than he did in Lincoln's Inn. In another party there was a man who had been a clergyman, in another a London lady's hairdresser who worked beside a Scot who swore he was a laird in Perthshire. It was as if someone took a giant dustpan and swept it full of the variegated inhabitants of the Three Kingdoms and emptied it in the Antipodes.

In all her existence Eliza was a girl who rarely ever had enough to eat. It is true that whilst at Madam Rose she was better fed, but there the work was hard and the hours long from early morning to late at night and she stayed in the dim light of the house and hardly ever went out. But on the Turon in the glorious Australian sunshine where the air was like wine and with as much plain but healthy food as she could eat she soon filled the hollows in her cheeks and put flesh on her bones. One night as she lay on her stretcher on a bright moonlight night, almost as bright as day, she felt her chest. There were two budding buttons under her fingers. She was on the way to becoming a woman.

*   *   *

One day not long before Christmas George's brother-in-law, Mr Lewis, appeared on the claim. He had a letter for George from Rolly.

"They are worried about you at Goonigal," he said. "Not a word from you and Christmas nearly here."

The letter from Rolly was full of reproach. Could George come back soon? Most of the men were away and there was a lot of work to be done.

"My word," said George. "I can't see how I can get away just yet. We're doing well on the claim and I can't leave me mates in the lurch."

Mr Lewis who had braved the bushrangers and the rough track and who rode over to the Turon for the purpose of seeing George was most disconcerted. However George gave him two hundred pounds to put in the bank which impressed Mr Lewis, for he was always impressed by money.

"You're doing all right, then?" he said as he wrote out a receipt.

George shrugged his shoulders.

"Well enough to stay here for a while."

Mr Lewis was introduced to the other mates, just up from the claim in their working clothes, stained with mud and dirt, and was served with a pannikin of black tea. Then he took the road back to Bathurst wondering what sort of gang of rough republicans George was associated with and where it would all lead.

And George went back to work and suddenly realised as he dug his shovel into the yielding gravel that for months now he had completely forgotten about his family. Goonigal and its people seemed in the far distant past. To go back to spending his days chasing cleanskins out of gullies or mustering scabby sheep or doing the thousand and one jobs needing to be done on the property now seemed quite ludicrous. Not for him the lonely plains of the outback after the busy, exciting life of the diggings. He told Mr Lewis he would write home and once or twice sat down with a pen and a piece of paper but no words came. So he forgot about it.

CHAPTER 9

Christmas time came with celebrations and then the New Year. With so many Scots on the field this day had to be a holiday and of course races were got up on the race course set on the hill above the town. What a crowd was there on New Year's Day! Eight or nine hundred people including some gentry from Bathurst, small settlers from around about with horses to race, a few shearers and drovers and a great crowd of diggers from Sofala and other places along the Turon. And there were all the other odds and ends of humanity that congregate on race courses; conjurors and thimble riggers, piemen hawking their wares and a few girls from Barrack Lane in Bathurst, looking for a good time and perhaps some custom.

It was Captain Bloomfield and other of the leading lights at the Sofala diggings who organised the meeting. The same mob, in fact, who set up the reception for the Governor when he came to visit the diggings earlier in the year. But the races were well put on, my word, with the judges and the secretary of the course and the two stewards rigged out in green corduroys and black top boots and both mounted on greys.

And there was a row of refreshment booths serving both food and drink along by the main stand, made of branches covered with canvas. The booths were surmounted either by the union jack or the green flag according to the nationality of the owner. Vehicles of every description poured in. Horses were led about by their grooms and groups of people picnicked on the ground.

When George heard there was to be a race meeting there was no holding him. It was months since he had ridden a horse and the smell of leather and the warm scent of horseflesh brought it all back to him. He had no animal to enter in a race but neverthe-less went to Sofala the day before the meeting and by talking to the right people and anyhow looking like a fellow accustomed to riding he arranged to ride one of Mr De Clouet's nags.

On New Year's Day George and his mates closed down the camp and left it to the care of a shaggy mongrel with ludicrous yellow eyes who was now attached to the party, considering no doubt that humans needed a good dog to look after them. George took the precaution of asking Mr Treganza to keep an eye on the camp, for the diggers were neighbourly people who helped their friends. The Cornishmen were resting as they were not racing people as this was a sinful pastime according to their Methodist way of thinking.

So George and Pat, the Major and Harry, all good racing people, with Eliza taking up the rear in a new dress she'd made for the occasion, took off for the races. It was a typical Australian day of early summer. The sky was a light Italian blue, the air was fresh and a gentle breeze caused the leaves to ripple in the eucalypts. In fact it was good to be alive, to be one with the great crowd of rough vigorous people all out to enjoy themselves.

"Ah," said Pat. "The man who doesn't like racing is a duffer!"

And for once the river flats were deserted, the cradles were silent and even the Sofala streets were empty as the crowd streamed uphill to the racecourse. There were three races in the morning and three more after the midday break to allow the refreshment tents to do their trading. In the second race George was to ride Mr De Clouet's *Larry the Gaff*, a fine chestnut mare. Leaving his friends at the rail George went over to where Mr De Clouet's horses were tied to a tree. *Larry the Gaff* eyed him affectionately as he fed her a piece of sugar and whispered in her ear.

When at last the bell rang for the race, an eight furlong event, George found four other horses lined up at the starting point. Next to him was *Romeo*, a black gelding mounted by Big Ben the horsebreaker, and next to him Harry the Boy on *Doublechalk*, then Red Mick from O'Connell on a backblock mare named *The Don*, then a brown mare called *Tom Boy*, mounted by a lad from some lost sheep run in the rough mountain country to the north of the Turon. The stewards lined them up and as soon as they were ready one shouted "Off!" and they were off and away with a rattle of hooves on the hard ground. *Doublechalk* went straight to the front, *The Don* followed him at a steady pace and then came George with *Romeo* on his quarter, rolling and weltering, with *Tom Boy* close behind. They swept up the dip like the wind, steadied at the turn and then came charging down the slope by now more spread out. The course was dry and hard and reasonably smooth. *Doublechalk* fell back and *The Don* was in the lead with *Larry the Gaff* half a length behind, and half a length behind him was *Tom Boy*, while *Romeo*, despite the efforts of his reckless rider was well in the rear.

With only one furlong to go George touched *Larry the Gaff* with the spurs and plied the whip. The horse came sailing through the ruck, overtaking *The Don* and leading by half a length. *Tom Boy* and his little mountain jockey came boldly up, overtaking the others, but failing to catch *Larry the Gaff* who came in first, a length in front. It was a good race and the crowd cheered like mad for it was known that George was a digger, the only digger riding that day which made him all the more popular.

But to George the smell of sweat and leather suddenly brought back to him a nostalgia for the great wide western plains where he used to ride in rough race meetings got up by station owners; where once or twice a year a score or two of people would foregather to see the wild bush horses compete against each other, while each station, differences between man and master forgotten, would cheer wildly for their nags. And then there would be the ride home across the darkling plain among the ragged trees until at last there would be a distant glimmer of light, a candle in the window of the home station. There would be enough to talk about for weeks after and someone would say: "Do you remember when our *Black Beauty* beat Mackenzie's *Silver Grey* and the old man was as mad as a cut snake?". Or perhaps some outsider would come in first or someone would take off for the bush because a couple of troopers appeared on the horizon, making a subject of conversation for months afterwards.

But George's thoughts were soon interrupted for at the refreshment tent were not only his mates but also Red Mick, Bob the Bumboatman, Big Ben the Breaker, Mr De Clouet and Mr Lee, both important people from Bathurst, and others who wanted to slap him on the back and buy him a drink. He'd won a wonderful race, they said and although his horse was good he'd brought it to the winning post like a master, a rider of judgement who knew how to get the best out of a mount. And so it went on, round after round of drinks.

The Major was off gambling somewhere, Harry was dead asleep under a tree and Pat was firmly settled at the Shamrock Inn with a mob of fellow Irish, so George and Eliza took the homeward track as the sun set over the dark hills. It was a warm, lovely evening and the beams of the setting sun sparkled in the dust haze hanging over Sofala village. They walked in the stillness down the track to Green Point.

"Let's go down to the river and have a splash," said George.

It was a good idea; both were hot and dusty. They crossed the pebbly strand and came to the river's edge in one of the few places where it managed at that time of year to run deep under the heavy crags of the northern bank. Both knelt by the edge and splashed water on their face and hands. The water was cool and relaxing. Eliza stood up and took off her shoes. Then she held up her skirt and paddled her bare feet in the cool water while George sat on the pebbles and watched her. It was almost dark now. Gaily she splashed water at him. Then she stepped on a greasy stone, lost balance and fell over backwards with a splash into the stream. For a moment she was held up by her clothes but they soon soaked up the water and she began to sink, drawn along by the current. She felt herself being carried away into the dark and slimy depths of the river, silent and sinister, and cried out for help.

George threw off his boots and plunged into the water. He had learned to swim with the Aborigine boys in the creek at Goonigal. In a moment he caught Eliza in his arms and waded back to shore. They clambered out, panting with the sudden exertion. He put her on her feet but she clung to him, still fearful of the bunyip haunted depths of the Turon that a moment ago threatened to drag her to her death. Pressed against him, her face against his chest, she could feel his heart beating strongly. He put his arms around her and pressed her to him, suddenly conscious of her warm little breasts pressed against his chest, of her soft thighs pressed against his muscular ones. He held her tight for a moment and then they separated, stood silent for a second and then walked back to the tent.

"I'm cold," she said, shivering. "I must go and change my clothes and get under the blankets."

She suddenly turned and kissed him on the lips and ran to disappear in the slip tent at the rear of the main one. George stood where he was, dripping water, rather bewildered, dazed by the feelings that rushed on him. His knowledge of women was limited — the wife of a neighbour who once drew him into bed with her when her husband was away, a girl in Barrack Lane one riotous evening in Bathurst. But Eliza was different. Hitherto she was a mate, someone you worked with, like Pat or the Major or Harry. But now that was changed. He visualised her standing naked in the tent, drying herself on the towel. He shook his head and sighed, went into his own tent, took of his wet clothes and lay on the bed, to drop at last into a sleep haunted by agitated dreams of flying through the air, of soaring and gliding through the clouds over the Turon.

*   *   *

The festivities ended, they all went back to work. Scarcely were a few tons of earth put through the long tom when Eliza came back from a shopping visit to Walberton with a copy of the Bathurst Free Press and her eyes popping out of her head.

"Everybody's talking about it," she said. "It's the new gold regulations!"

There in the paper was the news that the new gold regulations would be put into effect, including all the vicious clauses that hampered and aggravated the entire population of the goldfields. The thirty shilling monthly licence fee, the double fee for foreigners, a licence fee required for every person on the field regardless of whether they were digging for gold or not, the restriction on public houses and the particularly unpopular clause that required applicants for a licence to produce evidence that they left their previous employment with their master's permission.

This set tempers ablaze, for it was obviously the work of the tyrant Wentworth who wanted to drive free men back to the sheep runs.

The unrest on the field grew stronger, opinions became heated, commissioners were insulted to their face and over camp fires there were violent arguments about the course of action to be taken that lasted long into the night.

At George's camp there was general agreement that the regulations were unjust. But what to do about it? Harry Pole and the Major were both for leaving the Turon and trying their luck in Victoria, as the Port Phillip District was now called. Damn the Commissioner and his regulations! They'd try their luck somewhere else where the flats were greener and the claims richer.

But George thought they ought to stay on and see it out. They were on a good claim and sooner or later the opinions of the diggers would force a change in the regulations.

Pat was the most militant. He was a busy member of the diggers' association which was not only against the regulations but also opposed to the big mining companies that employed labour and machinery to work ground that by rights should be worked by the diggers themselves. At a Sofala gunsmith one day he purchased a Colt revolver of the newest model and sometimes went off into lonely gullies and fired practice shots. There were many among the diggers who had arms and some who talked of using them if the regulations were not changed.

Pat could neither read nor write; only once in his life had he been in a town and that was Bathurst which he passed through on his way to the Turon. His parents were convicts sent out in Brisbane's time. His father selected his mother as his wife from among the girls at the old female factory in Parramatta. Somehow, after years of work, old Ryan obtained several hundred acres of land in the wild mountain country to the south of Bathurst. It was mostly mountainside and rocky gullies where he ran wild looking cattle and some horses. On the few flat patches he grew a little wheat and some potatoes. Occasionally he disappeared for a week or two, to come home quietly at night. And then in the gullies were to be found cleanskins that were quickly branded and then sent off to the saleyards at Bathurst.

When the gold rush came old Ryan soon found ways of making money. There was a big demand for horses and cattle and whenever his potato crop was ripe he would fill a dray with sacks full and sell them for a pretty penny. Of his large family eight children survived to adulthood. There was a lad younger than Pat who still lived at home and there were four girls who married very early to young Currency lads of the district and two older boys of which one was out west somewhere and had not been heard of for a couple of years and another who was doing time at Cockatoo Island for stealing horses. Like their parents none of the children could read or write, firstly because there was no school where they could learn and it was anyhow not considered an accomplishment of great value.

The Ryans had plenty of friends of their own kind within a radius of fifty miles but they looked sideways whenever, and that was not very frequently, the troopers ventured into the area.

Old Ryan whose back was scarred by the floggings of the good old days had a strong dislike of authority, the police and anyone superior to him in wealth. He remembered dimly the days of his youth in Ireland, of fights between croppies and the police in which the peasants invariably lost, and of the English soldiers who helped the landlords to keep the land. These feelings were inculcated into his children. Pat went to the diggings because there was nothing much for him to do at home except work as an unpaid help for his father. When he arrived at the Turon he was struck with wonder. Never before had he seen so many people, so much excitement, so much activity. He also earned, even as a labourer, more money than he had ever had before in his young life and all earned by his own labour. At Christmas time he went back for a few days to his parents' slab and bark hut in Snake Gully. They were astonished at the presents he brought them from Bathurst and the tales he told of the diggings and of his mates. Back at the diggings he participated in the general hostility to the new gold regulations. He went to the meetings of the diggers' association and fell in with a group that used to gather every evening at an inn to talk things over. There was an English fellow who said he'd been a Chartist, a Frenchman who had fought on the barricades in 1848, a couple of Germans and two or three Irishman and even a couple of the native born.

They all had arms and talked headily about using them. When a protest meeting was organised they turned out in force to cheer and went talking among the other diggers on the field saying that the regulations should be resisted. This was a popular sentiment although the leaders seemed hesitant about any extreme action.

Oh, it was exciting to go through the diggings at night and by the red light of the camp fires to encourage the less enthusiastic, upbraid the recalcitrant and the timid. Pat helped to organise protest meetings and to obtain signatures for petitions, to find out who had arms and who didn't, who was prepared to stand in the front rank and who wasn't. He found all this highly stimulating. He found he was able to express himself with fair fluency and to hammer home to his listeners the basic facts of the diggers' argument — a ten shilling licence fee, no double fee for foreigners nor fee for traders; in fact more freedom for the diggers who were making the country wealthy despite the opposition of the wool and mutton lords. And, what is more, representation in parliament for the diggers!

However, he found his illiteracy a heavy burden. Finally he asked Eliza if she could help him, teach him his letters. Not that her knowledge was very great! However, in a month or two he could say his ABC and learned to decipher simple words. But there was never enough time. In the evenings he would tramp into Sofala, taking care not to fall into any of the unfenced holes that bordered the pathway, and in dingy back rooms in the flickering flames of camp fire would talk over the problems of the day. On Sundays he walked over the hills to little creeks where only a dozen or so diggers worked, to tell them his story.

It suddenly struck him that whenever he went to some outlying place there always seemed to be a trooper about somewhere, who might pass him on the track or from horseback on a distant sidling watch him as he went. In the committee of which he was a member there were half a dozen who were the most active. They met every two or three evenings to talk things over, to discuss the state of the diggings, the temper of the diggers and any movement at the commissioner's Camp.

The diggers fell into rough communities according to where they worked. There were those who dug in the immediate vicinity of Sofala, those at Golden Point, Pennyweight Flat, Wallaby Rocks, New Zealand Point and so on. In each locality they were bound by common ties. They would sometimes combine to divert the river channel, to dig a race, keep order among themselves, help a man down on his luck or a family which had lost a breadwinner through illness or accident. So it became customary for members of the committee to keep in touch with these communities, some of whom lived on distant creeks, many miles away.

Sometimes Pat went tramping over rough country as far as the Meroo, Tambaroora or Louisa Creek to take petitions for people to sign, and the people were always happy to see a new face and eager to talk about the injustice of the goldfields regulations. One day Pat mentioned to his friends on the committee the interest the troopers seemed to have in his movements. He found they suffered the same experience; the troopers were always watching them, asking to see their licences, sometimes searching their tents for illegal grog. When the meeting ended the Frenchman, whose name was Marius, took Pat aside and said:

"You know what this means. We have among us a mouchard, how you say, a spy."

"My Colonial oath! A spy on the committee?"

"But yes. How otherwise would they know who are who? Someone must tell them."

Pat was astonished. Did these things really happen? Marius took him to the Prospectors' Arms and they sat in a dingy back room and drank Colonial beer. Together they went over the members of the committee. There was Hans, the big German who loved music and sang songs of his own country with tears in his eyes. Marius shook his head.

"And Luciano?" asked Pat.

"No. In Italy he was a Garibaldino. He fought at Rome."

Pat did not know what this meant but said nothing to hide his ignorance. They discussed the other members of the committee.

"What about Sullivan?" asked Marius.

Sullivan, as his named indicated, was Irish, an ex-convict, an elderly man, big framed, a great beard turned grey, with a low forehead and bushy eyebrows. He was much against the authorities and spoke bitterly and vehemently, which brought him some prestige among the more angry diggers.

"Not Sullivan," said Pat. "He hates the commissioners.

Marius shrugged his shoulders.

"You never can tell," he said. Then he added:

"If there is a spy sometimes he must contact the Camp. He won't speak to the troopers, they are too stupid. Either he talks to one of the commissioners or perhaps to the sergeant-major. Therefore he goes to the Camp for certain after dark. If we watch we catch him."

So Marius and Pat took it in turns to watch the entrance to the Camp, or the Cantonment, as the commissioners called it. The Camp consisted of a slab building with a bark roof where the commissioners lived and a row of tents for the troopers. The whole was surrounded by a rough fence. There was usually a trooper on duty outside the slab building. For three evenings the two diggers took it in turn to watch from dusk until late in the evening. On the fourth evening Pat took it into his mind to watch a little longer. He sat in the shadow of a heap of earth musing when suddenly a dark, burley figure slipped through the gate in the fence. It was too dark to see who it was but who among the diggers would at that hour be going surreptitiously into the Camp? The figure disappeared among the tents. It was a pitch black night without a moon and only the stars blazed down from the cloudless sky. In Sofala across the river and along the banks were a few dim lights and the dying embers of the diggers' camp fires.

Pat waited silently by the track for fifteen or twenty minutes. It was now about eleven o'clock. Again a dim figure looked out of the darkness. It was impossible to see who it was so Pat approached silently as the figure left the Camp and turned onto the track.

"Is that you, Sullivan?" he called out.

The figure turned and stopped a moment and then darted off down the hill over the rough ground around Maitland Point. Pat tried to follow the sound of running steps and the rattle of stones but in the dark it was easy to lose one's foothold and fall into an abandoned pit or cutting. Sullivan, then, was the traitor? The Judas! A digger who betrayed his mates no doubt for money. Pat was filled with rage at the betrayal and with contempt and hatred for the traitor. His heart beat violently and the blood roared in his ears. He ran down the track towards the river, stopping now and then to peer into the darkness and listen for the sound of running feet. Sullivan's camp, he knew, was on the other side of the river and therefore to return home he must cross the Turon. Pat ran forward, keen and alert, like a hunting dog on a scent until he reached the ford. There he stopped and stood a moment and looked fiercely into the night.

A glimmer of light from a tavern door shone momentarily on a misty figure moving into the blackness.

Again Pat hastened forward and splashed across the shallow waters of the ford. Although he could no longer see Sullivan he could faintly hear the sound of rapid footsteps disappearing up the track that led to Lucky Point. This was a high and long neck of land around which the Turon twisted. The point was about a third of a mile long and two or three chains wide, surrounded on three sides by the river. It was known to the diggers as Lucky Point because the first prospector there had the luck to find a golden hole.

This bend in the river was a favourite place for bed claims that well rewarded their owners, so all around Lucky Point, which rose high above the river, were camps and cooking fires and by this time of night many sleeping diggers. Pat ran up the track that crossed Lucky Point at the base of the neck. He paused and could still here the sound of running, no doubt Sullivan pursued by his guilt. There was a fairly well defined track that ran along the top of the point and along this Pat sped like lightning. He was young, vigorous, full of righteous anger, eager to revenge a betrayal. Sullivan on the other hand was much older, tired, weary, guilty and frightened, almost a broken man. Within less than a minute Pat was right behind him, on him and caught him in a fierce grip. He could hear Sullivan panting with fear and fatigue and could feel his heart pounding in his chest.

"You dog!" cried Pat. "You Judas. You've sold us to the commissioners!"

He could feel Sullivan trembling with fear. He chattered something incomprehensible. Pat in disgust and hatred threw the man from him. If it had been daylight it would have been evident that they were both standing by the edge of a steep bank which fell thirty or forty feet to the river bed. Sullivan precipitated over the edge of bank fell with a scream into empty space. There came the sound of a body falling through bushes, a few stones falling down the slope and then silence, the silence of death. Pat stood still breathing heavily for a few moments. Then he turned and went grimly back down the track to the township.

CHAPTER 10

Among Donald Maclean's duties was that of being the coroner
for the district. It was for him to decide how died corpses
found rotting and putrid in the river or dried and mummified
in the bush or perhaps crushed to death in a fall of earth and
rock or who had broken the neck by falling in a big hole while
going home inebriated late at night. Then there were the people
killed in brawls or thrown from a horse or who departed this
life as a result of what was called in official terms "the visit-
ation of god". It was his duty to view the poor pathetic corpses
before he sat on the coroner's court and one day he was shown
a crumpled thing that went by the name of Patrick O'Sullivan.
He knew who O'Sullivan was and shrewdly suspected why he
was found at the bottom of the cliff, his head broken against
a boulder. However Donald returned a verdict of death from
unknown causes and the corpse was taken off to be interred
in the cemetery silently one evening by the hospital mortu-
ary attendant, without benefit of clergy, for no one knew the
deceased's religion although with a name like Sullivan he was
probably a Papist.

The next issue of the Bathurst Free Press carried a paragraph
which mentioned the event and added that the man's name was
said to be Sullivan although it was believed that his real name
was Gorman and that he was transported to the Colony in the
time of Governor Darling.

Donald carried out his coroner's duties conscientiously. This
was the sort of chore his colleagues were happy to leave to
him. They preferred to parade around the diggings catching un-
licensed diggers and hauling them off to the logs. The feeling
in the field worsened; the temper of the diggers was high. The
Scots diggers came to Donald and told him that the regulations
were unjust and caused much ill-feeling and that unruly elem-

ents among the diggers wanted strong action. He agreed with them and shook his head in despair. What was to be done?

Donald was an early riser and at dawn he would come out of his room and stand looking into the valley. Already smoke from early camp fires rose in the air and sometimes curtains of mist drifted up from the river. Gradually as the daylight illuminated the deep cleft of the valley the rattle of cradles began and a chatter of voices arose. Then added to the volume of noise was the clang of picks and shovels, the squeaks of the windlasses, the jingle and clink of carts and wheelbarrows, the barking of dogs and over all the gay shouts of the kookaburras greeting the day. Donald looked at the animated scene and wished he could find a more peaceful occupation than being in the Gold Commission force. He would probably be happier even working as a simple digger despite the hard work and the rough life and its precarious nature. But he needed some quiet occupation whereby he could lead a happy contented and useful life with Maria and raise a fine family that would be a consolation for him in his old age — for he was not young for a man about to embark on matrimony. But in these days there were few quiet places in the Colony, for due to the gold discovery it was as disturbed as an anthill a horse had trodden on.

Over the years Donald had built up a little nest egg and with his future brother-in-law's advice, Maria's marriage settlement and a loan from the bank he planned to buy a little property at King's Plains at present rather neglected but which could be substantially improved by hard work and which could provide a reasonable living for Maria and him despite the risks of flood, drought, falls in the price of wool and all the other hazards of Australian rural life. So when arrangements were more or less complete he went to Mr Green and handed him his resignation. The worthy Commissioner looked grim and handed it back and said that in view of the situation on the Turon goldfield it was impossible for Mr Maclean to leave for some time.

"The extreme agitation among the diggers over the goldfield regulations may burst into violence at any minute, " he said.

"We know that at least four hundred men are armed and ready for action. I am bringing all the available troopers here as soon as possible and I have sent to Mr Deas Thomson asking for a party of the Eleventh Regiment to be dispatched to the Turon."

Mr Green frowned.

"The diggers are better organised than we think and I am sure the man Sullivan who supplied us with information and on who you held an inquest yesterday was really murdered by the diggers, although how and by whom we do not know."

So against his will Donald agreed to postpone his resignation for a month or two in view of the Commissioner's wishes, but that he would be granted two weeks' furlough to enable him to be married. So it was and a little before Christmas he went back to his lodgings in Bathurst. Two days later he and Maria were married at the Duncan homestead by the Reverend Mr McOarts of the Free Church of Scotland. Donald drove his wife back to his lodging where his bachelor's single bed had been replaced by a comfortable double one for the occasion. It was felt that the bride and groom should spend the first few days of their marriage by themselves.

The next morning Maria was happy to awake with the thought that she was no longer a maiden but could face the world with a man she could call her own. Maria was a simple enough soul brought up in an environment where women were only concerned with their husbands, their home and their children. In this sphere they were expected to be happy and contented and so they were, providing they had a good husband, one who did not get drunk and beat them, carrying on with other women or lose their livelihood as a result of gambling, speculation or the low price of wool. Maria considered her father to be a good husband; he behaved with respect to his dull little wife, never drank too much and worked hard. Most of the Scots settlers were honest and hard-working people bound to respectability by ties of family and nationality and the Kirk and if any of them stepped from the narrow path it was with discretion.

But it was not thus with other settlers as Maria well knew. There were the Randalls, Anglo-Irish gentry, very high and mighty, and Randall, a man of fifty who had a good property and a substantial income would now and again get roaring drunk, beat his wife and flog his twenty year old daughter because he suspected she was carrying on with the son of a neighbour.

Once, she heard, he had a mad fit and shot all the does and threw them in a haystack and set fire to it. Then there was poor Mrs Haddon who was a lady but who lived in a little cottage and took in sewing. Her husband was English gentry sent out to the colony with money in the hope that he would settle down. But he spent most of his time in the Royal Hotel with drunkards and gamblers and various dubious women. He would come home late at night all in liquor and jovial and then slap his wife's face because she didn't welcome him. At some time in his life he caught a disease and one of the children was born deformed, like a little monkey, but luckily didn't live long. Haddon became more and more peculiar and when his creditors began to close in one morning went down to the stables and blew his brains out.

And the women of the lower classes — their fate was even worse! At thirty they were worn out by childbirth and household drudgery and by forty looked old, tired women. So often their husbands were afflicted by the terrible Colonial adoration of the rum bottle and when drunk beat them black, and blue. And sometimes the women took refuge in drink and ruined their health and looks with the square black bottles of rum. Then husbands would be accidently killed or maimed and women would be left penniless with children to feed and dependent upon the bleak winds of charity. And there was a recent case in town of a man who in a drunken frenzy threw his wife and three children out of the house on a cold winter day and refused to support them.

Maria looked at the people around her and thought how lucky she was. She was brought up in a house where the only voice raised in anger was that of her father and no one took his bad temper very seriously, for it was soon over. Her mother was a distant, rather reserved person but nevertheless Maria had a happy childhood. She was a favourite of her father and of the farm servants, mostly old Highlanders, shepherds who despite their years in the Colony never learned properly to speak the Saxon language. Her father spoke Gaelic to them and she and her brother acquired a little of the language. Maria was educated at a little school run by two old spinsters. Her brother being a man and therefore more important went to Dr Lang's Australian College. Maria was taught to read and write and do simple arithmetic and also to sew, to play the piano and to paint.in water-colours, of which she made an awful mess. Reading she took to at an early age. When her father was really old he became immersed in religion and the house was full of books of sermons and other religious works, and fiction was frowned upon as something rather sinful. Walter Scott's novels were permitted and she would drown herself in them, dreaming of Scotland, that distant but noble and romantic country whence her family came. Then she would borrow books from her friends and in secret read novels by Dickens and Thackery and Bulwer Lytton and others at night in her bedroom, by candle light when everyone else was asleep.

She had of course her work. She was given charge of the dairy, making cream and butter and she looked after the poultry — chickens, ducks and even a flock of geese. To help her she had the inevitable Irish orphan girl, poor little Mary Murphy, an ignorant Papist who could neither read nor write and was as honest as the day and devoted to Maria.

Although she was born in Scotland, Maria was so long in the Colony that she spoke with a tinge of the flat Colonial accent to the annoyance of her mother, who affected the English way of talking despite her Irish origin. Her family were once grand landowners in Ireland and her father, Mr Derwent, had owned a great property at Carakooleen. Her parents were dead but she had one sister married to a legal gentleman in Dublin and another who went to Canada, so she said.

When Maria passed her twentieth birthday and her girlhood was behind her, thoughts turned to marriage. There were quite a few suitors but they were either too poor or too English or two Irish for her mother or too unattractive for Maria. Her social life was limited to a rare trip to Sydney, the weekly Sunday journey to the Bathurst Kirk, an occasional shopping trip to Mr Webb's store during the week, a tea party at the home of some substantial settler, a dinner party or a ball to celebrate someone's marriage or other event. But now all that was behind her. She had her husband, her Donald, and at night she would clasp her arms about his rough, muscular body and press her face into the hair on his manly chest, to send him into a flame of passionate desire that needed her willing co-operation in the quenching.

A few days after the marriage Donald and Maria returned to the Duncan house. One afternoon they set out on horseback (for Maria was an excellent horsewoman) to ride to King's Plains to inspect the home they would go to as soon as Donald was free. It was a small but well-watered property and should respond to good care. ,They would take with them one of the Duncan shepherds, Old Rob, to look after the sheep, and Mary the Irish Orphan, so devoted to Maria and who would help in the house and the farmyard. The house was small but could be added to. But it was a home, their first home, near enough to Maria's mother when advice or assistance was needed and not near enough for that good lady to interfere in the family arrangements.

In the late afternoon they took the homeward track. There were good rains that Spring and the rolling hills were rich with grass. The sky was a pastel blue and the sinking sun shone through light floating clouds that sailed gaily across the horizon. The landscape gave off an air of rich and pleasant calm. Lazy crows watched the two riders from tree top perches, magpies chortled in the grass, bush turkeys took off with a rush and a flutter from their hiding places and a mob of kangaroos feeding among the trees pricked up their ears, glanced keenly at the riders and bounced off into the distance. It was a beautiful and touching scene. Donald turned to his new wife and held out his hand to her. She brushed back the whisp of auburn hair that perpetually fell across her cheek, clasped his outstretched hand and smiled tenderly at him.

The sun was setting as they rode back to the Duncan home. It fell below the western horizon in cascades of red and purple, foretelling of a fine day on the morrow. When at last they reached the Duncan homestead there was a trooper's nag tied up outside. Inside was the trooper with a letter from Mr Green. It was to Mr Maclean requesting him to return to Sofala the next day and to bring a detachment of troopers waiting at Bathurst. Things were not good, wrote Mr Green, and he feared that in a day or two there might be trouble.

CHAPTER 11

John Murdoch mounted the royal mail coach to Bathurst at its starting point — the Black Boy Inn at the corner of George and King Street. It was the most expensive but the best way of travelling to the goldfields for, as the name implied, it carried the mails. And with all the thousands of new people away at the diggings, the mail service was inundated with letters. It was a good coach with four horses and only took five passengers. The drivers were the best in the Colony and assured a reasonably safe journey. The coach left at five o'clock in the afternoon and arrived at Mr Rotton's hotel in Bathurst at six the following evening, all being well.

The coach started off with a cheer from the passers-by and rattled up the badly paved street, past the cemetery and then downhill towards the Haymarket. As the coach passed Goulburn Street John looked out of the window. There was at the corner a slim form wrapped in a shawl who waved to him. This was Alice, come to bid him goodbye. He waved back and she was soon out of sight. Mr Bowden who was also travelling to the Turon so both could investigate the potential riches of the Ajax Quartz Vein Company looked at him curiously. He was aware that young Murdoch had a liaison with some woman, and this evidently was her.

John stretched his legs and lay back on the rather uncomfortable leather bench seat. He was pleasantly relaxed and a little tired. That day he did not go to work but hired a gig and he and Alice drove along the South Head Road to a point overlooking the Harbour with a delightful view of green hills, yellow beaches and pastel blue seas. They ate a lunch of cold fowl and drank a bottle of white wine. Then they returned to Alice's room and lay on the bed for the rest of the afternoon and made sacrifices to Venus to propitiate the gods so that Johnnie would come safely back. Alice wept and clung to him when he left to collect his baggage and go to the coach and she promised to wave to him as he went past the corner of the street. This she did and watched the coach disappear along the road to Parramatta. Her heart sank and she felt lonely and abandoned, empty and weary, despite John's promise of fidelity. So she went back to the house and made a cup of tea. She was very happy to be able to give herself so entirely to John but behind the happiness was always the gnawing worry of what the future might hold. How glad she was to have escaped from Madam Rose! When in London she first became a prostitute whatever she did with men was less important than the money it brought her. She could at least eat as often and as much as she liked, drink as much Mother's Ruin as she wanted, buy new and fancy clothes and cheap jewellery, have a roof over her head and have some sort of security. And for love she had her Cockney pickpocket. Then came her illness and the voyage to Australia. Even before she met Johnnie she had begun to turn against the life in College Street. Rolling on a bed with all manner of men who treated her at best with indifference and often with contempt and hatred became more and more repugnant. But how to escape?

Then Johnnie came and with him it was different. At last came a chance to escape, the first step towards a new life. Now she felt that the layers of her old life and outlook had been peeled away and she was down to her true self. That evening she sat at the window watching the passers-by until the quick Australian dusk fell, and mused on what life might hold for her. Johnnie loved her, she knew, and he found strength in the association. But how long would it last? Alice, after all, was but a prostitute taken from a brothel—a kept woman with no rights who might be abandoned as soon as he tired of her. She was scarcely eighteen and there was much life ahead. Since she lived in the Colony her health had improved and she had become a good-looking young woman with a comely face and figure. Johnnie was so evidently attached to her that she sometimes wondered if he would ever suggest marriage. But there were insuperable difficulties in this. How could he present her to the McFees, the Bowdens and the other well-to-do merchant families? She could just about read and write, she couldn't embroider or paint in watercolours as ladies were supposed to do. In a town like Sydney where everybody knew everyone there were sure to be questions about her origin. And she might meet in society someone who had met her at Madam Rose's place and perhaps even gone to bed with her. There were too many embarrassing possibilities. And respectable women! She knew with what bitterness they hated those who left the narrow path of virtue. She felt John would not abandon her — certainly not for a while. But he might be taken ill, even have an accident and be killed in the wild diggings. Then she would be left to fend for herself and at the moment there was only one alternative, to go back to Madam Rose. Since she broke with the life of prostitution she now held it in abhorrence. In the street one day she met Annie who told her that Margaret was drinking herself to death and Madam Rose was talking of expelling her from the house. Mary was in the hospital, victim of a disease that made her a danger to the clients. Alice knew the inevitable fate of girls who went on the batter, caught in a circle which ended in drink or disease or both.

There was one alternative and that was to find some sort of work. But even for straight girls there was not much to do — to work as domestic servants or in a shop, perhaps. However, the next day she enquired around and found a woman who employed a few girls at dressmaking. Alice's ability in this field was limited and she could only do the most primitive work and sweep up the shop and run messages for long hours at a pittance. Still with the money John gave her she had enough to live on and what she earned she put aside. Also she was learning some sort of occupation that might at least enable her to survive if the worst came to the worst.

*   *   *

The coach rattled along the road to Parramatta where it arrived a little more than an hour after it left Sydney and where the horses were changed. The sun was now settling in a vast red and purple conflagration to the west and the night fell suddenly. There was no moon and no light except from the feeble glimmer from the coach lanterns shining faintly on the dusty, bumpy road ahead. Occasionally they passed a dimly lit cottage and sometimes ghostly eucalypts loomed out of the dark. Apart from John Murdoch and Mr Bowden there were three other passengers — a settler and his wife going home after a visit to Sydney, and a merchant on his way to Bathurst. About nine o'clock the ford at Emu Plains was reached and they stopped for a bite of supper before they crossed the river and with fresh horses began the long climb up the mountains. For the rest of the night the passengers dozed fitfully, awakened only when the coach stopped at some wayside inn to change horses, where even in the depths of the night a noggin was always available. At last the grey glimmer of dawn came through the dusty windows. They stopped at another staging place and tumbled out all tired and grimy and stiff from sitting up all night in hard seats. At that moment the sun burst up on the eastern sky and revealed before them was a great vista of rolling olive-green mountains with ragged red cliffs and deep tree fringed valleys. It was a vast, romantic landscape the like of which John had never seen before, that left him breathless, in awe, at the strange almost unearthly wonder of it; the wild magnificence of the view that opened to the westward. The others stretched and yawned and grumbled and Mr Bowden called to him to come to the inn for breakfast. The air was as fresh as wine and he gulped great lungfuls of it. He felt as if he was in a way new-born, in a new-born landscape, so different from the bedraggled, dull littoral plain and the untidy, crude little town and its rough people that clung to the coastline. The vehicle rattled on all day. It took hours to climb the steep pinch at Mount Lambie. Finally, when they seemed to have reached the last stage of exhaustion, the coach arrived at Bathurst not long after six o'clock and came to a stop before Mr Rotton's hotel. It was already dark and both John Murdoch and Mr Bowden were exhausted. They required no more than a brief meal and then to roll into bed for they were to take the coach to Sofala at eight the next morning.

*   *   *

They were late arriving at Sofala for the coach lost a wheel at Wyagdon Hill and it was necessary to bring a wheelwright from Peel to repair it. Mr Tregoning met them but it was too late to go on to the mine. So next day they travelled on horseback through deep, bush covered valleys and up great hills to a vast lonely plateau where you could see for miles and the air was as clear as crystal. To John whose previous was of the soft green hills and distant purple mountains of Ulster or the arid pastel colours of the Colony's coastal plain, it was all wonderful. Wonderful too was the excitement of the digging, the thousands of people hurrying to and fro, of the babble of many tongues and the rattle of cradles. Also the thought that he was now engaged on an exciting enterprise, for the discovery of gold caused an immense advance to the Colony and would advance it still more.

Along the track they occasionally passed bearded travellers, sometimes diggers going to a new location where the prospects were better, sometimes just travelling with no apparent object in view. Mr Tregoning looked at the travellers with his gimlet eye and then loosened the new revolver he wore in his belt. Although it was spring the weather was cool and there were big clouds that raced across the sky and a sharp wind that shook the straggling branches of the ragged eucalypts. They came at last to a sharp ridge overlooking the deep Turon valley. Here there was a camp — a couple of tents and a rough, newly constructed bark hut. It was midday and there were three men having a spell, eating meat and damper and drinking black tea. When the horses were unsaddled and some food consumed Mr Tregonning took them down the ridge a little and showed them a line of white quartz outcrops.

"This is the reef," he said. "It strikes in an almost north-south direction."

He then took them a few yards farther down to where there was a pile of broken earth and stone.

"The men have sunk a shaft here. We took out some samples and dollied them and found good colour. Now we are driving an adit into the side of the hill to find out how deep the vein runs."

He was full of enthusiasm. His little black eyes shone with eagerness and he waved his arms as he spoke of the gold that could be won. He was almost overcome with the thought that in a desperate battle with nature he could bring the earth's secret riches to the light of day. There were three wages men at work now, he said, and he proposed that more should be put on, or better still experienced miners brought from Chile where he had worked himself for many years in the copper mines. He could speak the language and knew their ways. They would also be uncontaminated by the restlessness that effected the other diggers on the Turon and would not have the terrible desire for higher wages so typical of the Colonial. Then a stamping battery must be obtained. He could design one and in Sydney there were workshops that could build it. A steam engine would have to be brought over the mountains, too. It might be six months before the mine would be in proper operation. The area was a choice one, he considered. A lease was already applied for. If they did not take up the site then someone else would, perhaps one of the other mining companies now operating in the area. Mr Tregoning was very enthusiastic indeed.

Some of the enthusiasm rubbed off on John. It was Mr Bowden's intention to spend a couple of days at Quartz Reef and then return to Bathurst where he had business with Mr Lewis about promoting the company's shares among those in the district with money to invest. John however decided to stay longer at the mine to learn something of the workings and also to examine the country more carefully, even going as far as Tambaroora where another reef mining company was set up.

Truth be known Mr Bowden, a man of over fifty years of age, accustomed to easy living, found the travelling somewhat exhausting, the accommodation crude and the goldfields in general too rough and brutal for his taste. He insisted on John accompanying him back to Sofala as he feared that alone he might be held up on the way by bushrangers. So off they went on their hired nags, John armed with Mr Tregoning's new Colt revolver, although he had never fired one in his life; but at least the sight of it might frighten away evil doers. After seeing Mr Bowden on to the Bathurst coach John mounted his horse and rode up river, past Erskine Island, up Ration Hill and on to the village of Walberton. As far as he could see parties were working the river flats although the level of the water was running low, just making a trickle over the pebbles. He continued on past Pennyweight Flat, over Scabby Hill and as far as Green Point where the track crossed the river and went up a long ridge called the Razorback and finally led, he was told, to the main road from Sydney to Mudgee. But he turned his horse at the river and went back to Walberton where at an inn he lunched off bread and cheese and Colonial beer and talked to the diggers about their luck.

Then he rode back to Sofala and as he neared the town came up with one of the assistant commissioners, a tall fair haired young gentleman who rode with a cavalry seat. Behind him were three mounted troopers and in between them walked half-a-dozen diggers manacled to a chain, evidently taken for not having a current licence. The scene, thought John, was repulsive; the haughty, arrogant fellow on horseback, the surly troopers and the pathetic, dejected diggers tramping along with unhappy, downcast faces.

John shivered and let the party pass him. Then he rode back to the town and spent the rest of the day inspecting the mining operations around Maitland Point. He took a room at the Prospectors Arms and then, it being late in the afternoon, made a tour of inspection of the town. There were several public houses, he noted, and three churches, an Episcopalian, a little Catholic chapel and a wattle-and-daub Methodist structure. The clergyman's house was a slab hut behind the chapel yard. John, who wanted someone of his own kind to talk to, knocked on the door and introduced himself to the resident minister, a Mr Piddington. He was made very welcome and invited in for a cup of tea, out of a china cup and not a pannikin, for Mr Piddington rarely saw others than rough diggers. Mr Piddington was a rather pathetic man, grey faced and weary, who came from Yorkshire. It was very hard on the Turon, he said. God was forgotten in the lust for gold. Apart from some Cornish miners and one or two shopkeepers, few came to the church. The other clergy could tell the same story, even the Papist priest, Father O'Connell. Sofala was full of drunkenness and the sins of the flesh. He sometimes did not know which way to turn, so awful was the sinfulness around him. Why, only the previous evening a man had disembowelled a woman with a shearing blade. He was drunk and so was she but she lingered on for hours in the most dreadful agony. It was awful. But, he said, the majority of the diggers were not really bad men but led astray from the path of the Lord by lust and greed.

And there was growing trouble with the authorities, he said. The goldfield regulations were manifestly unjust and led to much friction. That very afternoon Mr Waterford, the assistant commissioner, had arrested six diggers for not having licences. Four of them were unable to pay the fine and would go to Bathurst gaol for fourteen days. Two of these, a father and son, left behind a girl of eighteen, the daughter, without protection and almost penniless. Mr Piddington said he did not know what to do. He felt that the law must be upheld but the regulations were so evidently unjust that perhaps the diggers after all had right on their side. He looked around his mean little hut. Life was difficult, he said. He came here to bring a message from the Lord but few were prepared to listen.

*   *   *

John Murdoch spent four more days on the Turon, travelling as far as Tambaroora to visit the various points and creeks where men were digging and to climb the steep hill to see the new Sergeant's quartz mine where a number of men were employed underground and a mill was set up to crush the quartz. Then he returned to Quartz Ridge and found that Mr Tregoning had collared in a shaft and set up a windlass. He was on the vein, he said, and when the right machinery was available they would all make their fortunes. In the meanwhile he would set up a Simple Mexican crusher and probably produce enough gold to pay wages.

At last it was time to go back to Sydney. John took a deep breath of the sparkling air and mounted his horse. He waved goodbye to Mr Tregoning and trotted off along the rough track that led to Sofala. As he ambled up the hills and down the gullies, for he was in no hurry and enjoyed the keep mountain air he turned over in his mind the events of the last few days. The search for gold he found enormously stimulating and far more exciting than the tedious business of commerce, as the invigorating air of the Turon was to the heavy humidity of Sydney Town. To search for the nimble pennyweight, to fly on the wallaby track, as the diggers said, seeking the golden metal, to mix with wild, strange and fearsome people, come from who knew where, far from the routine of the cash book and the journal, the dull Sunday sermons and even duller Sunday suppers of Mrs McFee — ah, this was the life, the real life! He determined that on his return to Sydney he would buy or borrow books on geology and mining, so as really to study the subject. The gold discovery had already transformed the Colony, and wasn't there also copper mining in South Australia and even around Bathurst? Mr Tregoning said that in a few years the diggers would come to the end of the alluvial deposits, but there was plenty more gold in the quartz reefs that abounded everywhere, but needed machinery and capital and wage workers to be released from the rock. He looked at the rolling hills covered with thick bush, at the Turon trickling placidly at the bottom of the valley. Where, oh where, was the gold hidden? Under what great heap of rock did it lie awaiting for man the magician to release it? In fact the bluff he was traversing at that moment might contain vast wealth or, more likely, mere sterile country rock. How to know? Here knowledge was needed and he was determined to acquire all the knowledge he could on the subject on his return to the coast. He felt he had a talent for the industry, that he could play a great part in it. Time would show. The afternoon was coming to an end as he ambled over the hill at Lucky Point and dropped down into Sofala where the lights were already beginning to twinkle.

Suddenly he remembered! Alice before he left Sydney asked him to see if he could find trace of her little sister Eliza, supposed to be somewhere on the Turon. Alice! Since leaving Sydney he had scarcely thought of her — the goldfields had fully occupied his mind. It suddenly came upon him that he was fallen into a situation contrary to all the standards in which he was brought up. He had a sinful relationship with a girl of the streets, a common prostitute! In the eyes of the church he was a man who had committed a mortal sin which endangered his afterlife. Was he in effect damned, with all the devils in hell at his heels? John could see the respectable people of Sydney pointing a finger at him — a sinner! What would the future hold for him if his present entanglement continued? Without finding an answer to the question he stabled his horse, then took a cup of tea with Mr Piddington who was as desperate and pathetic as ever and very despondent about the situation on the Turon.

He told John that a clash between the diggers and the authorities was inevitable unless the goldfield regulations were altered. He urged John to tell the responsible people in Sydney that something must be done or there would be trouble. And he invited him to a prayer meeting to be held that evening to be attended by a few of the more devout and God fearing people of the town.

John departed, promising to return but somehow the earnestness of the little man repelled him, and the subjection of self to an all-powerful God, before whom humans were but little more than sparrows made him shiver. At the Prince of Wales Inn that evening John fell in with a party of successful diggers and spent the whole evening imbibing rum and talking about the advantages of this or that method or the value of this or that creek or flat or dry digging. He forgot all about the prayer meeting and by midnight staggered to bed where he collapsed into a. deep and rum soaked sleep.

CHAPTER 12

Many stupid things took place as a result of the irrational government gold regulations and which only served to exacerbate the miners. Now it happened that the claim holders in the part of the Turon surrounded on three sides by the neck of land called Lucky Point came together and worked out a scheme to keep the river water out of their claims. There were about three hundred of them and they agreed to pay five pounds each to have a tunnel driven through a narrow part of the neck somewhere near where Sullivan or Gorman, as some called him, fell to his death. Thus the river water would be diverted through the tunnel and hundreds of yards of the river bed made available to the diggers. So a contractor, a Mr Colquhon, was given the work. He decided he needed a dozen workmen to work an eight hour shift three shifts a day and he hoped to break through to the other side in about six weeks. They were all ready to start when one of the assistant commissioners appeared. Mr Drake said the workmen would have to pay the thirty shillings a month licence fee. But they were not digging for gold, said Mr Colquhon. No matter, they were on the goldfield so they would have to pay for a licence. He wouldn't listen to any argument. That was the end of the matter as far as he was concerned. Either the fee was paid or the men would be arrested and fined. This meant that Mr Colquhon was obliged to pay the licence fee himself, which made a big increase in the cost. He argued that when the tunnel was driven three hundred bed claims would be worked producing more wealth for the miners and more money for the government. But the assistant commissioner's face was blank. Such talk passed right over his head. He was only concerned with the regulations, and according to the regulations the licence had to be paid for.

And as a result of this, the generality of diggers concluded that the commissioners were not only men who hated the diggers but that they were also excessively stupid. This was all the more trying because the weather was very dry and the river really reduced to a trickle. The flies were terrible and half the diggers suffered from the sandy blight. All four in George's party developed the irritation and Eliza rubbed their eyes with Holloway's ointment every evening.

It was the height of summer and in the valley the heat was oppressive. The great whinstone cliffs glowered down on the diggers labouring in the river bed, cursing and grinding their teeth at the heat, the flies and the lack of water. And these were the people the commissioners went out of their way to annoy and frustrate with the ridiculous and bureaucratic regulations! At a time when the river bed was laid bare by the receding river waters and the diggers could reach places hitherto untouched, there was scarcely any water with which to wash the pay dirt. What water was flowing was sticky and yellow and full of unmentionable filth. George and his mates were weary to death but the claim they were on was a real golden hole. They worked it to the fullest extent for it was well below flood level and a big down-pour of the kind so frequently found on the Turon could see the whole thing washed away.

They would sometimes look up at the trees that stood near the river and see bits of grass and leaves and other rubbish caught in high branches and estimate the number of feet of water that would cover the claim if the river really ran a banker.

But every evening they gathered in the stuffy little tend and looked at the heap of yellow grains and water worn nuggets. Every evening there were four or five ounces and occasionally as many as fifteen or twenty. No doubt about it, they were making a pile and there was a great heap of wash dirt lying in the paddock for which at present there was scarcely enough water to wash. At the bottom of the shaft, now about twenty five or thirty feet deep, they drove in one direction under the gutter for about forty feet. Then they came back and drove downstream. They were about thirty feet along the gutter and getting good values. Down below in the drive it was hot and foetid and the stagnant air made breathing difficult. The drive was dimly lit by a candle on a piece of wood stuck into the wall. It was customary for the men to change jobs every hour, so arduous was the work. The drive was only about four feet high and those working in it had to scramble about awkwardly on all fours. While one was working at the face another filled raw hide buckets with dirt and dragged them to the bottom of the shaft where they were hooked to a rope and then hauled up to the brace by the man at the windlass. He tipped them over the edge, pay dirt to one side, mullock to the other. The drive on the advice of Mr Treganza was roughly timbered with stulls supporting cap pieces and longitudinal lagging covered with bark to prevent small stones and sand from falling on the men at work. The party ran out of timber and this meant a day's work in the bush to out and drag it back to the camp. There seemed to be more urgent things to do at that moment and as the ground appeared pretty good the last ten feet of the drive was left through the naked alluvium, held up by its own cohesion.

One day about the middle of January, in fact the day after the first big protest meeting at Mr Ashe's sale yards, Eliza was by the tent cutting up damper for the men's midday meal. Pat was repairing the cradle, Harry was hauling up buckets of washing stuff and the Major and George were working below. Suddenly Eliza heard a rumble and a thud and the whoosh of a great volume of air rushing up the shaft and sending a vast cloud of dust into the bright midday sunlight.

There must be a collapse in the drive! She knew George was below and her heart sank and a terrible fear gripped her. She clasped her hands over her mouth and her eyes starting from her head she ran towards the claim. At the same time Harry ran to the brace where Pat was standing half blinded by the dust, his hands to his eyes. Everyone within earshot looked up and many hurried towards the scene, for when a digger is in trouble his fellows always stood by him and came to his help, such was the comradeship of the goldfields.

Treganza was the first to arrive and he and Harry went down the rough ladder tacked to the side of the shaft. They found George at the bottom half stunned and blinded by dirt. Treganza produced a candle and lit it and crawled up the drive. About twenty feet on he found it blocked by fallen stones and river gravel. But the Major's head and shoulders protruded from the heap and although unconscious he was still breathing. He must have heard the ground beginning to give and tried to get back but was caught by the fall.

In the meantime someone helped George out of the shaft and sent down a shovel and some buckets. Oh, how glad Eliza was to see George emerge from the shaft dusty but alive and unhurt. She led him back to the camp and found water to wash the dust from his eyes and face. After long and arduous efforts Treganza and Harry managed to free the Major from the fall. On his left leg was a heavy rock which had to be checked and levered off with a crowbar, Then they carefully drew him along the drive to the bottom of the shaft. They put a rope under his armpits and those above gently turned the windlass. At the same time George climbed up the ladder to steady him as he rose in the air and to prevent him bumping against the sides of the shaft. The Major hung from the rope like a dead man, his head on one side, his deadly pale face smeared with dirt and his arms dangling. His crushed, crooked left leg oozed blood through the cloth of his trousers. At the brace the diggers lifted him gently and laid him on a rough stretcher and he was carried to the tent.

At Walberton there was a medical man, a Doctor Johnstone, not unpopular with the diggers. The title of doctor, of course, was a courtesy one, for he was really only an apothecary, or even an apothecary's assistant who had found his way to the Colony and then to the diggings where no questions were asked about credentials. Nevertheless he was a hardworking little man who did his best for his patients and who had a good practice experience of sprains and breaks and all the ills the diggers were given to.

He came hurrying along on his old nag to Green Point and cut the torn trouser off the Major's leg, looked at the crushed and twisted flesh and shook his head. The Major stirred and half opened his eyes, muttered something and relapsed into unconsciousness. Doctor Johnstone rubbed his hands on a dirty handkerchief and said that the patient would have to be taken to the hospital for further treatment. Everyone looked uneasy for they knew this meant an amputation and perhaps the end of the Major's life as a digger. It was a good four miles to Sofala and the doctor said he would be off to prepare things. Two sets of diggers carried the Major along the track, each set of four taking turns with the stretcher. Eliza came along behind with some clean clothes. As they passed Golden Point the Major woke up and cried out in pain and moaned and groaned and muttered incoherently until the hospital was at last reached.

Doctor Johnstone, practical and no fool, had seen many amputated limbs turn gangrenous and the patient die after horrible suffering. But back in Portsmouth where he learned his apothecary's trade he remembered old sailors, veterans of Nelson's fleet, with only one arm or one leg but still as healthy as rabbits. They told him how when their limb was crushed by a grapeshot or a falling spar the surgeon would saw it off and cover the stump with boiling tar. This made you faint with the pain but nevertheless the wound would heal clean and the patient would survive to beg for a living in the streets of Portsmouth. So when Doctor Johnstone amputated, even if he didn't wash his hands, he at least cauterised the stump well and truly before bandaging it. And for reasons which he did not understand his patients usually survived — as long as they did not die of shock.

It was his custom to operate after filling his patients with rum and laudanum, tying them to the table and helped by a couple of hefty men to hold them down, to hack and saw away. He was quite expert and could have a leg off in about thirty seconds. But now he had a new invention, one of great benefit to humanity. This was a liquid called chloroform of which a bottle was recently sent to him from Sydney and which he now intended to use for the first time on the Turon, probably for the first time west of the Blue Mountains. The Major was conscious by the time he arrived at the hospital although still deadly pale and moaning with pain. He was taken into a room and laid upon a table. There was Doctor Johnstone in his shirtsleeves and on a bench were scalpels and a saw all shiny and bright. The poor Major showed the whites of his eyes.

"My leg, my leg," he cried for he knew now that it was to be cut off.

But the good doctor restrained him and placed over his face a cloth that reeked of a sickly, sweet-smelling odour. "Breathe deeply," the Major heard someone say and then everything seemed to go around and around and he felt as if he was being impelled at a mad speed down a long pipe.

*   *   *

The Major's friends sat outside the hospital on a bench while Doctor Johnstone laid bare the shattered leg above the knee and rapidly sawed through the bone. The rough wardsman took the leg, boot and all, wrapped it in a cloth and went away with the poor bundle to the furnace at the back of the hospital where such things were burned. Then the Major's friends smelt the sizzling flesh as the Doctor cauterised the bleeding stump. At last the Major was bandaged, wrapped in a blanket, taken to the long ward and laid on a bed. After a while he awoke. Around him, watching anxiously, were George, Pat and Harry with Eliza.

Some colour came back into the Major's ashen cheeks and he smiled a little to see his friends again and he muttered a few words of thanks. Then he said:

"Oh, my leg, it hurts."

Then he started to mutter, for his mind was wandering and he finally fell asleep. Silently his companions left the room and went along the weary track back to Green Point.

*　　　*　　　*

The Major took the loss of his leg fairly philosophically. He lay back in his bed smoking his short black pipe and staring at the ceiling. Each day one of his mates or else Eliza walked from Green Point to see him. The hospital built with the money subscribed by the diggers and the Sofala shopkeepers was well enough run, the food was rough but ample and now and then Doctor Johnstone looked in to see how his patient was faring. He was happy to note that no infection of the leg followed the amputation. The use of chloroform for the first time on the Turon brought him some fame, with a little of the glory reflected on the Major. In fact people came into the ward just to look at him: the man who had his leg off under chloroform!

The Major signed and puffed his pipe and a rough old wardsman brought him a tray of food. With profound melancholy he put down his pipe and consumed the mutton broth placed before him. What, in fact, did he now have to look forward to? With only one leg there was little he could do on the digging except perhaps rock a cradle and be a burden to his mates. How was he to live in the future? Of course, he thought, the situation he was in was the result of his own folly, of following his own whims and desires without thought. Lost and crippled in this distant God-forsaken colony, surrounded by rough people, ignorant, rebellious democrats, far from people of his own class, what could the future hold for him? If it was not for his predilection for gambling, the excitement it gave him to win or lose at a game of cards, or to bet on which side of a coin tossed in the air would fall upwards, he would still be riding at the head of his squadron to the clatter of horses hooves and the rattle of accoutrement. He knew he was a good soldier, a competent officer. Ah, if only there had been a war to take him away from the terrible temptations of peace! But the debt mounted up and the debtors became more pressing and then there was the matter of a big loss at cards that he just could not meet. The scandal became so great that he sold his commission and took the first ship he could get out of the Port of London, which happened to be going to Australia. And on board he chummed up with Harry sent off to the colonies to get him out of the way because he got some village girl with child. So no more for the Major were the merry parties, visits to the girls in the Haymarket, then breakfasting on bacon and eggs and hock and seltzer. He was still considering his dismal future when Eliza appeared at the door bringing him the best wishes of his mates, some fresh food, a flask of rum and a little spray of the strange, faded native flowers that grew on the slopes of the Turon valley.

*   *   *

Pat was a participant in organising the big meeting at Mr Ashe's sale yards on January the fifteenth when over a thousand diggers assembled and a giant petition with nearly two thousand signatures protesting against the gold regulations was taken to the Camp for submission to the Governor in Sydney. The Commissioner received the petition quite calmly and treated the delegates with good manners. As the end of January grew near the excitement mounted. On February the first the new gold regulations would come into force. The group in which Pat was involved was all for not paying and resisting any attempt at digger hunting, and by force if necessary. All the river there were several hundred men armed and determined to fight. Frightened shopkeepers at Sofala told the Camp that diggers were buying large quantities of gunpowder. There was in fact a sullen, smouldering fire on the Turon which would not need much to fan into a consuming flame which might engulf them all, as Mr Green wrote to the Colonial Secretary in Sydney.

At Green Point George and his friends sat and considered the situation. It would take at least a month before the Major was well enough to come out of hospital and some time more before he was fully recovered and fitted with a wooden leg. Even then he would not be able to work as before. So in the meantime they washed as well as they could the heap of gold-bearing dirt already mined. The claim in fact was pretty well worked out and it was time to move elsewhere. George already had his eye on a likely piece of ground about half a mile further up the river. Anyhow, with the water level as it was it would take two or three weeks to wash the dirt. But such was the strong feeling among the diggers that almost anything could happen in that time. It was a crucial period for the Turon.

This was indeed true. On February the first, the day the new gold regulations became legal, there was a great meeting on Sofala Flat with about a thousand people present. Pat was on the platform because he was now one of the prominent men in the diggers' association and before he knew what was happening the chairman, Mr Maxwell, announced that he was to address the diggers. This brought a cheer from the crowd for Pat was already known to them. He stood up. embarrassed, not quite knowing what to say. But then he looked at the sea of bearded, sunburned faces and words came to him:

"Turon miners!" he said. "On the first of February the Government is going to enforce or try to enforce a set of regulations which is fit only for a nation of tyrants and slaves. These regulations are intended to drive all hard working diggers from the mines and make them slaves at ten pounds a year for the settlers. If you submit to being treated like this without striking a blow for your rights you deserve to be slaves. Now is the moment to prove yourselves worthy of the rights of free men. Every Point on the Turon can turn out from one to two hundred armed men and what can the commissioners oppose to this? Arm yourselves with guns, pistols, knives, picks and shovels and surely the miners can beat the constables and the commissioners. Let us stand to our rights like men for if we are beaten who knows what tyrannical act may come next. Let us not be conquered by a handful of police for if we are we deserve to be treated like dogs and slaves. And you may depend upon it, we shall be. His blood be on his own head who tries to oppress an industrious and peaceful body of men!"

Pat stood back exhausted. There were cheers and shouts from the crowd. In a corner of the Flat a dummy representing William Charles Wentworth was set up on a pole and put fire to and burned to ashes amid the jeers and delight of the crowd. Then the meeting broke up.

*   *   *

Mr Green sat in his hot and stuffy office in the Camp puffing a cigar. He was recently arrived from Bathurst at the head of a dozen mounted police and paraded through the main street of Sofala to impress upon the diggers the extent of the armed might of the camp. There were now about thirty troopers and foot police which was far from enough in view of the situation. A week previously Mr Green had dispatched a message to outlying districts to send all available men to Sofala. Also to the Colonial Secretary in Sydney he wrote a report stressing the gravity of the situation and asking that a detachment of troops of at least half a company be sent to the Turon. The arrival of a body of trained soldiers would make no doubt about victory if there was an outburst. If left to the police the outcome could be disaster. They would be immediately overcome and the Turon would be in the hands of the rebels. The Boston Tea Party all over again.

Mr Green had in his hands a document which served to confirm his worse fears. It was a leaflet passed around among the diggers and which had come into the hands of the Commissioner through an agent in the diggers' ranks. It began:

"Their Excellencies the Diggers in General hereby give notice that on the first of February next the following regulations will be enforced against all commissioners, policemen and other ruffians of that kind. Firstly: Any commissioner asking for a licence is declared an enemy of the people, liable to shooting, hanging or other violent death as the diggers may determine. Second: any policeman, trap or peeler who attempts to take into custody any free and independent digger shall be ducked three times in the river, stripped of his livery and pelted with stones for the space of an hour. Third: a sergeant to receive double. Fourth: Every Point to form an association for the protection of the men working on the said point. Fifth: Any men who will not join the association who pays a licence to be struck off the books and receive ten lashes for his cowardice. Strike, miners of the Turon, strike for your rights!"

These violent and revolutionary sentiments, that struck at the heart of civilised society, filled Mr Green with horror. Combined with the sort of speeches made at the meeting on the Flat, it showed what sort of a situation he was faced with!

*   *   *

As the Major once remarked, Mr Green was an autocrat by habit, education and circumstance. Like most autocrats he was a lonely man. He was all the more lonely in that he was faced with a difficult situation, with limited means to deal with it and with subordinates in whom he had little confidence. His assistant commissioners, Drake and Waterford, behaved as if they had the entire British army at their backs instead of a score or so of hapless troopers who would be more likely to take to the bush than to stand if faced with a mob of diggers with their blood up. Then there was Maclean, a reliable and sensible fellow, but whose heart was not in the business. All he wanted was to go back to his wife and get into bed with her and who had been persuaded with difficulty to postpone his resignation from the force. The only man in whom the Commissioner had any confidence was Dogherty, the sergeant major, a pretty competent fellow. If he had been a Frenchman in Napoleon's time by now he'd be a general of division instead of a warrant officer — but that was not how things worked in British countries. The spirit of the diggers! This was the most important thing to judge. As far as the Commissioner could find out there were two main parties — the physical force people and the moral force lot. The latter were usually better off than the former, and included most of the known leaders, such as Mr Maxwell and Mr Majoribanks. They were tenacious in their own way but would not go against the law nor oppose by force the collection of the licence fee. However the physical force boys were much more demanding. As the proclamation showed they were prepared to use force to prevent the collection of the licence fees. This would inevitably lead to bloodshed and once the diggers tasted blood they would drive the troopers away. They knew what they wanted and would stick at nothing to get it. A gang of revolutionaries, many of them foreigners and Irish. Mr Green had the English gentleman's dislike of aliens and the Irish, particularly if they were Papists. He also knew more than a little about what was going on and despite the death of Sullivan still had his agents inside the diggers' association, although they were rather more discreet than in the past. Recently some of the physical force boys thought the better of the situation and went off to Victoria — perhaps fearful that things might go farther than they were ready for. The main physical force man was John Smith, a dark little Welshman who had worked in the coal mines in that country. Then there was a Captain Muller who asserted that he was once an officer in the Prussian army. Recently had come to the fore the native born fellow named Ryan, but full of Irish bitterness and rebellion. A regular trouble maker. Mr Green sat in his hut, smoked a cigar and drank a glass of port and cursed the wretched diggers. He wished gold was never discovered and that he was back at his property at Rock Forest cultivating his sheep in the company of his handsome wife. What a pity that despite much attention to the subject by both of then she had never had any children.

And he cursed the diggers and the gang of agitators, foreigners, Chartists and socialists who led them, the troopers, the assistant commissioners, the mosquitos, the heat and the bad food. He went to the door of his hut and looked at the valley. It was a bright moonlight night and the giant moon hung low in the sky, its brilliance illuminating the scene before him. One could almost see to read a book so bright was the light, although the shadows were as dark as ink. The valley of the Turon lay at his feet, dark and sinister, with the lights of Sofala and the diggers' camp fires scattered like diamonds along the river bank. Away to the west he could see the bulk of Wallaby Rocks rising darkly on the horizon. He ground his cigar into the earth, went inside to undress and lie on the camp bed under a mosquito net, cursing the stifling summer heat until he fell asleep.

CHAPTER 13

Oh, what a turmoil there was in the Colony when the new gold regulations were announced! In the stuffy summer heat of Sydney the liberals and radicals cursed the squatters for being blind to reality and trying to keep the place as a sheep run, a nursery for the production of wool. They pointed out the example of Victoria where millions of ounces of gold were being dug out of the ground, where in not much more than a year Melbourne had grown from a sleepy village into a thriving metropolis. The squatters ranted and raved but the diggers, the rough democrats, were making thousands of pounds and the merchants and banker millions. Gold, in fact, was a wonderful thing. Whoever owned it was lord of all his wants. It had no smell, no nationality, no religion, no opinions but it brought men from the ends of the earth to this lost and lonely colony to make their fortune or die in the attempt.

One day Roland, looking over his sunlit plains frying in the heat, thought it was time he saw some more of the outside world. His wealth was increasing, partly by selling cattle at high prices, partly by a rise in the price of wool. He could afford a month in Sydney for his family, staying at Petty's Hotel. And on the way he would stay in Bathurst for a while, with his brother-in-law. While in Sydney he wanted to see the Lands Department about leases farther out. Leases for a couple of runs which he would stock and put under competent management with perhaps Chinese coolies to do the work.

So early one morning they all set out along the track south, Rolly on his big black mare, Betty, Amelia, the two children and her female servant Jane in a cart and each night they camped and slept under the stars, a great adventure for the elder child, Ernest, who lay and gazed in wonder at the star lit heavens. Not long before they reached Bathurst they passed a band of rough looking working men and Rolly asked them if they were in search of work for he was always in need of hands at Goon-igal. They asked him how much he was likely to pay and he told them; — ten shillings a week and rations. They looked at him for a few moments and then burst out laughing

"Hey, old fellow," said one. "We've just made a pile on the Turon and now we're off to Ballarat to make another. We won't be working for you, but we might buy your run and put you in as a manager."

They laughed to see the look on Rolly's face. Then one wit said:

"We're short of a cook, old fellow. You can have the job if you like."

Then they went on their way laughing uproariously, leaving Rolly red-faced and fuming with anger. This event made Amelia realise how much she had grown to hate the Colony. When she looked at the harsh landscape, the bedraggled trees, the intense sunlight, she felt an alien, a stranger in this lonely, arid land. How she longed for the sweet meadows of Wiltshire, the placid avenues of trees, the rich abundant countryside, where the common people were polite and respectful to the masters and did not stare rudely in your face, as they did here. And where was the good society, tea parties, little card parties, pleasant country houses and majestic cathedrals. She sighed as the cart jolted down the rough track. True her husband was wealthy and likely to be more so but there was a shadow on her soul and at the moment she would have gladly traded it all for some pleasant country cottage near some quiet cathedral town. Australia, she thought, was a place fit only to make money in, a place for migrants.

"In these days," remarked Amelia to her husband when they reached Bathurst, "brawn and muscle are the new aristocrats. There is no respect for worth and talent or education and good breeding."

She hoped the Colony would not be ruined as a habitable place for civilised people.

However the stay in Bathurst proved an opportunity for Amelia to meet people of her own class, for out on the Bogan they were few and far between. So she and her sister-in-law went visiting among respectable people in the town. At tea parties in the afternoon she heard talk about the latest fashions from England, the latest in mantles, brocaded and flounced dresses, embroidered merino robes, bonnets made of velvet, plus, silk or straw. And the other subject of conversation was the eternal one of the Colony, one that concerned the ladies of Bathurst ever since there were ladies there — the subject of female servants. These were a Colonial nuisance — insolent, dirty, immoral, particularly the Irish. And since the discovery of gold they had become very haughty and imperious. It was agreed that they were overpaid, overfed and uneducated. They typified the flood of ignorance and prejudice that had overtaken the Colony since the discovery of gold.

The first thing that Rolly did when he settled his family into Mr Lewis' home was to go for a walk through the town. The last time he saw Bathurst it was a sleepy settlement in the bush; now it was crammed with people. There was a theatre where Mr Howson performed with his party or where the Ethiopian Serenaders entertained the diggers. Then there was the migrant barracks full of Irish Orphan girls eager to marry a digger or a small settler rather than be a slavey in the house of a gentleman settler. There were the sly grog shops and the little houses in Barrack Lane where the girls stood by the doorways and beckoned men inside. By the evening the town was full of drunken men and women and the police, the blue uniformed charlies, not always very sober themselves, weakly attempting to keep order. And up and down the dusty streets flocked travellers, either just up from Sydney and bound for the Turon, or else boarded diggers in cabbage tree hats on the way from the Turon to the newly opened diggings on the Ovens River in the Port Phillip District where, it was said, gold could be picked up like mushrooms.

Rolly found the situation not unexciting although he heartily disapproved of the diggings and felt that they undermined the foundations of society. What he did find disturbing was that the town merchants and professional people were all in favour of gold and had already held a meeting of protest against the new gold regulations! Even Mr Lewis wanted the regulations changed. More, some of the settlers who now made money by selling cattle and sheep to Turon butchers said the gold discovery was the best thing that ever happened to the Colony. Rolly went to see Jamie Dunbar whom he had known since they were both boys together at school and Jamie told him how he was letting out river flats to small settlers so they could cultivate vegetables and other produce that found a ready market on the Turon. Rolly shook his head at this. His idea of a gentleman was a person who ran sheep on broad acres and live a settled, patriarchal life.

Rolly felt it was time he did something about George. He was worried about the boy. He had a strong sense of family responsibility and he didn't like to think that his younger brother was off on his own, perhaps mixing with dubious people. Nevertheless the boy could not be doing so badly for there were two hundred pounds to his credit at the Bank. What was the future for the boy if he stayed on the diggings? Rolly mentally referred to his younger brother as a "boy", although the "boy" was a grown man. There was no doubt that the general contempt for order and personal appearance, the crowding together of great numbers of rough people without decent accommodation, the smoking, the swearing and drinking must all tend to weaken the regard for external decencies and impair the sense of self-respect which, as Amelia said, is the foundation of manners and morals in civilised life.

But, as Amelia also pointed out, this rough gold digging life was not for people like the Bartons. Besides, as everyone said, the gold would not last and already the Ophir field was almost exhausted. The Colony would inevitably return to growing wool, for which it was intended. The squatters' time would come again, land would tell in the long term. Perhaps George could be set up on a run somewhere out west, she said, for he was always good with sheep. But before that why not take him to Sydney for a change where he could meet people of his own class and perhaps be influenced for the better by them. Since Mr Lewis' last visit to the Turon there had been no news of the lad although he had promised to write. Times were troubled, too, on the Turon, with all the arguments about the gold regulations. Mr Lewis had some banking business to transact at Sofala and Rolly not only wanted to see George but also to find out what the famous goldfields really looked like. So one hot summer morning when the distant purple ranges shimmered in the heat and the sun poured its rays fiercely down from the Italian blue sky they set off on horseback along the track that wound over the plains and hills to the great battlements of Wyagdon. By the middle of the afternoon they passed through Wattle Flat and began to descend the long and steep pinch to Sofala. They rode through the town which to Rolly's eyes looked like a great gipsy encampment and took rooms at the best hotel, the Prince of Wales, a timber and bark structure that boasted thirteen rooms for guests.

Rolly at once rode over the ford to the Camp to pay his respects to Mr Green, who received him politely but seemed preoccupied and said that things were rather tense on the goldfields at that moment. Rolly told him he came to see his younger brother who was working on the field and had last been heard of at Green Point. Mr Green said he understood that the young man was still working a claim at the same place. He smoothed his moustache and added that confidentially he understood that while Mr Barton's brother was well thought, of some of his associates were engaged in the agitation against the current gold regulations. He stroked his moustache again and said:

"Quite frankly, Mr Barton, and speaking confidentially, the gold regulations are quite unrealistic and will only lead to trouble. The Legislative Council will be sooner or later obliged to change them. In the meantime of course, law and order have to be maintained and one cannot let the mob dictate to authority."

Rolly left the camp with a feeling of unease. It was too late to go to Green Point. However he walked around the town and looked at the strange and to him distasteful variety of people in the streets and adjoined to the Prince of Wales with Mr Lewis. There they ate a fair dinner and talked with one or two gentlemen until it was time for bed. Sleep, however, was disturbed by the sounds of revelry that lasted late into the night.

Next morning which was bright with sunlight but heavy with summer heat they set out on horseback and after an hour's ride descended Scabby Hill to the ford at Green Point. Here they found George and his two companions cradling dirt in the droughty trickle of the Turon River. The meeting was scarcely a success. George and Roland were glad to see each other, it was true, and George was happy to have news from home. But hardly had Rolly been introduced to Harry and Pat and to little Eliza than he took his brother aside and told him that he must leave the diggings for there was sure to be trouble over the regulations. Why not come for a holiday to Sydney? The brothers looked very alike standing by the river's edge with the light green of Scabby Hill on the one side and the dark bush that covered the whinstone crags on the other. But George was quite determined. He said he couldn't possibly leave his mates on the lurch and one was still in hospital as the result of an accident. Besides, they had done well out of this claim and planned to open up another farther upstream. So after a rather stilted conversation and a pint of black tea served in a pannikin by Eliza Mr Lewis said it was time they left as he had business to transact in Sofala and Mr Barton anyhow really ought to see the diggings downstream. Before they left George gave Mr Lewis another two hundred pounds to put in the bank for him. Rolly was astonished.

"Why;" he said, "the Commissioner only gets five hundred pounds a year and now you're earning nearly that in less than six months!"

George laughed and his companions smiled.

"The difference is," he said, "that I earn my money by hard work. I don't get money for bothering people who only want to earn a crust."

Rolly started to reply but felt there was no point in pursuing the subject. Nevertheless it made him realise that there was a big gap between George's attitude and his own; his brother was won over to the digger way of thinking. Mr Lewis was already beginning to feel uncomfortable in this nest of brigands. So off they went, after George promised to write and also as soon as he could get away to come to Goonigal to see his father who was far from well.

As Rolly's nag ambled up Scabby Hill he felt that it might be best not to say too much in Bathurst about what his brother was doing. After all, gentlemen didn't go to the diggings, except for some eccentrics who came from England for unknown reasons and had no other means of subsistence. He thought about George's companions. Harry Pole was a gentleman, of course, but a weak creature obviously sent to the Colony to be rid of. Ryan, on the other hand, was a dangerous and determined man and the Commissioner was right to be wary of him. There was the traditional Papist trouble-maker! Full of discord, always against authority, ignorant and no doubt superstitious, ready to defy authority, probably capable of anything. Like those in Ireland during the recent famine who were given money to buy food by English philanthropists but who bought arms instead. Let it be hoped that he would not lead George into trouble with the authorities. There was the girl. A healthy creature now, obviously devoted to the men and particularly to George. But it would not be long before she was an adult and in that case she would be more of a danger than the turbulent Ryan. Fancy having her as a sister in law! What would Amelia think?

*   *   *

The first few days of February passed and there was no sign from the Camp. The cunning Mr Green sat tight and did not say a word, nor try to collect a licence fee. He was biding his time for although he now had fifty mounted troopers he knew that this was not enough in the event of a collision with hundreds of angry diggers. Also there was half a company of the Eleventh Regiment on the way from Sydney, at that moment sweating its way up the incline of the Blue Mountains. When Mr Green had sufficient force at his disposal he would act but not before. In the meantime every day parties of diggers left for Victoria. They were worried about the possibility of trouble and said they had come to New South Wales to dig for gold, not to battle with the commissioners. Besides there was hardly enough water in the river to wash the dirt.

Pat Ryan was again about the diggings with a petition. He asked the miners to sign a statement to say that they would not pay the licence fee until the regulations were altered. The more determined willingly signed and other did so because they feared not to go along with the majority or that they might be called cowards by their mates. Mr Green's agents among the diggers reported the growing part played by Ryan in the protest movement and how he attracted the support of many who previously were of the moral force persuasion. This set the Commissioner thinking and he had a long talk with the sergeant major. A few days later as Pat was walking along by Erskine Flat in the direction of Sofala he was approached by a couple of troopers on foot.

"Where is youse goin'," said one roughly.

"Where I'm goin' is my business," replied Pat tersely.

"None of your lip, now," said the other trooper. "Or you'll be off to the logs."

Pat always short tempered where the police were concerned turned on them his eyes flashing, his fists clenched.

"Now then," he said. "what do you two long nosed mongrels want with me?"

"That's no way to speak to one of Her Majesty's troopers," said the bigger of the two. And he thrust his big ugly face into Pat's and said:

"Keep a civil tongue in your head, you low Irish bastard!"

At this insult Pat hit the trooper on the nose and tumbled him backwards on the track. He was about to face up to the other when a third appeared from behind a heap of mullock and pinioned him by the arms. He was in a trap! He had fallen for the oldest of provocations. He almost burst with rage and pushed himself violently backwards. Pat and the trooper fell on the ground, Pat on top blowing all the wind out of the fellow's lungs and leaving him gasping. The first trooper sprang forward but Pat hit him fair in the stomach, doubling him up. While the three men struggled to their feet, groping for their sabres, Pat ran off like the wind up the track to Green Point and was out of sight before the troopers were able to gather their wits about them.

At Green Point Pat told his mates of what had happened. Harry was astonished. To dispute with the police was something outside his knowledge, and George stared in amazement. But Eliza knew the score. She knew all about police having dodged the peelers in London many a time. With her quick Cockney acuteness she got the measure of the situation.

"You can't stay here, Pat," she said. "They'll be along in no time. Pack up a blanket and I'll get some tucker for you and be off to the hills across the river to hide."

And how right was her judgement! Scarcely ten minutes after Pat had gone a party of two mounted troopers headed by Mr Waterford clattered down Scabby Hill.

"Hey, you, my good man," said Mr Waterford to George in an abrupt tone, "Is Patrick Ryan here?"

"No," said George in a steely tone.

Eliza piped up:

"We aint seen 'im since this morning, when he went off to Sofala."

Mr Waterford ignored her. He motioned to one of his troopers.

"Look in that tent."

The trooper dismounted and walked towards the tent. Like many quiet people George was capable of moments of intense emotion. At Mr Waterford's remark he felt anger rise in him like a tide. His muscles tightened and he looked at the assistant commissioner with an expression of such violent hatred that the trooper halted.

"If you go into that tent," said George slowly and distinctly, "I'll break your neck."

The trooper's mouth dropped open and he looked at George with frightened eyes. Mr Waterford swore and put his hand on his sabre which he began to draw from the scabbard. He bent over his horse's neck towards George and said:

"Damn you, that's no way to talk to my men. What do you mean by it?"

The last sentence he practically shouted. Then George walked over to Mr Waterford, put his hand on the sabre hilt and shoved it back in the scabbard.

"Mr Waterford," he said slowly and with great intensity of feeling, "If you care to get off your horse I'll give you a threshing and throw you in the river."

Faced with six feet of muscular native born humanity Mr Waterford suddenly came back to earth. It struck him that George was quite capable of carrying out the threat regardless of the consequences. He paused for a moment then jabbed his spurs in the horse's flanks and rode off with a scatter of stones, the two troopers following him. Waterford cursed to himself. Colonials and diggers! how he hated them! When he arrived back at the camp he made no mention of the incident to Mr Green although the event soon became known among the diggers and added considerably to George's prestige.

*　　　*　　　*

So Pat was no longer able to take part in the diggers struggle in public although he went surreptitiously among them at night, for there was a reward out for his apprehension. He wondered if he should go back to his father's place and lie up for a while. But the relations between the diggers and the commissioners were becoming more tense and after having spent so much time and energy in Sofala he was reluctant to leave. So he stayed on hiding in the bush by day and moving about only by night.

CHAPTER 14

John Murdoch returned to Sydney his head in a whirl. As the coach rattled along the final stretch of road from Parramatta to Sydney he tried to decide what to do next. First in his mind was his relationship with Alice. He was beginning to think that it was a relationship into which he had slipped almost unknowingly. Should he leave her and return to a life of moral rectitude? But what would happen to her then? It was obvious that she would have no alternative but to go back to the life she lived previously. Yet this was, he knew, the solution the McFees and others of their kind would consider the right one. By the time the coach at last reached the Black Boy Inn he still had not decided on the course to take. So he shrugged his shoulders and gave a boy sixpence to carry his bag back to his lodgings in Castlereagh Street. It was late in the afternoon and he sat in the darkening room his head in his hands. How could he go to Alice and tell her they must part? He knew what a protracted and painful scene there would be. And he could not say that he did not love he for if he was true to himself then he did. Knowing her had made a man of him, turned him from a bit of a ninny into an energetic man capable of action and decision. She had helped to develop his character, to bring out strengths previously covered by timidity and fear. This he admitted to himself. Suddenly the path of righteousness, so acceptable to the McFees and Mr Scope, the Methodist minister they frequented, appeared dry and arid like a track through a desert. In his mind's eye he saw their grim faces, expressive of self-satisfaction and so lacking in mercy for the transgressor. And the McFee girls! He would surely be expected to marry one of them. He sighed. He was nevertheless filled with doubts as to the road he should take. He had a long report to write for the Ajax Quartz Vein Company directors, complete with recommendations for future action. Now he was tired. He would arise early next morning and start on it before breakfast.

*　　*　　*

John found Sydney still in a turmoil. This dusty, dirty, muddy, drunken and licentious city of seventy thousand people, where everyone knew everyone else's business, was still in the great state of excitation engendered by the gold rush. Gold was always the everlasting subject of conversation. People arrived by ship at Port Jackson almost every day and everyday people from a score of countries could be found travelling by one means or another up the rough track that went by the name of the Western Road. In the Sydney streets people gathered around shop windows that displayed gold nuggets or large bits of quartz with gold embedded in them. And other shops were filled with the thousand and one items required on the goldfields by the diggers — or so the advertisements said.

People who remembered Sydney in the old days would say: "Ah, you wouldn't know the place. How it's changed! You'd think you were in another world, so dull and sleepy it was, and only eighteen months ago."

So the turmoil spread and fermented from the great Colonial mansions of Potts Point and Macquarie Street to the miserable tenements and dilapidated slum houses of Durand's Alley or The Rocks. And the squatter lords and the Government House mob nursed their hatred of the present day and dreamed of the good old times now gone for ever. Now they said the country was finally and completely ruined for without shepherds at twenty five pounds a year the sheep would be eaten by the wild native dogs. It was impossible to shear them for lack of labour, which would result in the destruction of the great wool industry upon which the country was based. But they would not listen when their opponents pointed out that the price of sheep was more than doubled, that horses and cattle were well up and the value of squatting stations was increased as much as four times. And the sheep did just as well without shepherds and seemed to survive quite satisfactorily all by themselves.

There was money in the town now, so much money, more than ever before and the squatters, the merchants and even the shop-keepers and tavern keepers and some of the common people had money to spend as never before. On Sunday after church well-to-do people rode out in their carriages dressed in the latest English fashions; the men in broadcloth coats and beaver hats, rather uncomfortable when the temperature was about thirty five degrees Celsius, while the women were wrapped in petticoats and camisoles, with crinolines, hats, bonnets, mantles, satin flounces and lavender boots.

*   *   *

To the ordinary people of the town drinking and fighting were favourite amusements and in the narrow streets that stank of excrement men and women lay drunk and unconscious in the gutter and people walked past them, even stepping over the bodies without paying attention, as if it was the most natural thing in the world. The town was full of diggers down for a holiday, spending their money right and left, drinking champagne and wine, throwing nuggets on the bar counter, eating six course dinners at the Gold Diggers Arms in Pitt Street and then in gangs full of food and drink and good fellowship go off shouting and singing to establishments such as those of Madam Rose in College Street or the less reputable brothels in Woolloomooloo of which there were said to be over forty. Amongst the drunkenness and debauchery, the violence, murder and robbery there were still people whose thoughts extended beyond the next noggin or hearty meal or profitable speculation. There were charitable people who helped the destitute and the sick, people like Dr Lan, who dreamed of freedom and independence for the golden lags of Australia, people like Deniehy or Parkes who thought of a better future for the country, or serious minded working men, masons or cabinet makers, who considered forming associations to better their interests and help make for themselves and their families a better life.

And everywhere there were discussions about the new constitution, for the squatters were fighting to hold their grip of the country, a grip which was slipping, even if they still held on to the reins of government, even if the debauched Governor and the canny tight-faced Colonial Secretary were in their pockets. John Murdoch told Mr McFee that as a result of the gold discovery the diggers were already levelling past distinctions and the centre of the country's wealth was moving from the sheep's back to the mines. The day of Australia as a sheep run for the Wentworths and their friends was ending. And the thick-headed stupidity of the Government was likely to cause a clash between the diggers and the authorities which could benefit no one. There were two factors to consider, said John. Firstly as a result of the gold a class of merchants, bankers and capitalists now existed full of energy and determination, who wanted the country to be more than just a sheep run. Secondly there was a large body of diggers, men of sinew accustomed to gaining a living by their own hands. When the alluvial terrain was exhausted of gold they would certainly not go tailing sheep for squatters. Perhaps some would find wages work in the new reef mines now being developed. But the big demand would be for opening up the land for small settlers, which would inevitably mitigate against the squatters. So the coming period would be one of turbulence, he said. The next year, 1853, would see a big struggle firstly over the obnoxious goldfield regulations and in Sydney over the new constitution. John's opinion, which he represented forcefully, caused consternation to Mr McFee, Mr Bowden and the other directors of the Ajax company. They were in half a mind about things, for they lent money to the squatters, also they marketed their produce, yet at the same time they wanted more freedom and more mining.

But John impressed upon them that the gold rush presented great opportunities both in mining and in serving the great new market opened up by the big increase in population. Reef mining was beyond the means of the ordinary digger but it was an opportunity for the investor who could provide capital to buy machinery and employ labour. But the unreasonable goldfield regulations must be changed for they were an impediment to the free development of the Colony. It was no longer a producer of wool and tallow but a gold producer with all the trade and industry that mining required.

As John left the office that evening one of the clerks handed him a letter. It was from Mr Scobe asking him to visit Mr Scobe's home in the Glebe in the afternoon of the next day. John felt as if a hand had come out and gripped his heart. He knew only too well why Mr Scobe wished to see him. A moment before he had been full of enthusiasm, proud of the way in which he had presented his case to a group of astute men of affairs who were obviously impressed by his ability. He had come a long way since he came to the Colony and he could go farther. Yet there was a problem to be overcome — the problem of Alice, that filled him with guilt and remorse. What was he to do? He left the building still clutching the letter. The sun was setting over Darling Harbour in a riot of red and purple, and the reflection of the violent colours shimmered in the dark, still waters of the bay.

CHAPTER 15

The situation on the Turon grew more tense and strained. Mr Green still sat grimly in the Camp, looking down on the township spread out before him, watching the diggers working their cradles and long toms, all quite illegal, for that month only a few timid ones paid the licence fee. Mr Green knew that the next day a monster meeting of protest would be held on Sofala Flat. At last his inaction had goaded the diggers into doing something, and the meeting was to be a deliberate attempt to challenge the power of the Commissioner. So far that February he made no attempt to collect licence fees, for Mr Green did not wish to provoke a collision. The time was not yet ripe; the party from the Eleventh Regiment was on the way at last at the regulation pace that carried it twenty miles a day and it would be still some more days before the half-company reached the valley. He glanced up at the Union Jack that hung disconsolate in the hot afternoon sun. The time when accounts must be settled was coming near.

*   *   *

The digger leaders habitually met in a private room at the Prospectors Arms. The landlord was a firm supporter, or said he was, and perhaps he was for there had so far been no attempt to interfere with them. So on the eighth of February they assembled there to discuss what they should do at the great meeting to be held the following day. The worthy Mr Maxwell favoured passing a resolution of loyalty to the Throne and organising a petition to the Governor. In this he was supported by some, but Donnolly and Pat, and Marius who was there to represent the foreign diggers on the field, were strongly in opposition. They sat around the table smoking short black pipes, pots of Colonial beer in front of them. The room was filled with tobacco smoke and was dimly lit by the thin flame of a lamp. The men were rough looking, hardened by labour, with faces deeply tanned by the sun and the wind. All gripped their pots with big work swollen hands. Mr Majoribanks was indignant about the leaflet the diggers had hand written and posted on trees along the river.

"We'll spoil our case," he said. "I'm a loyal subject of the Queen. As loyal as anyone. All I want to do is to work in peace. The Governor must be made to realise this. And putting up inflammatory posters will only stir up trouble. If we put our case reasonably I'm sure we'll be listened to."

Mr Maxwell agreed with these sentiments and was half-heartedly supported by others.

"The Governor!" exclaimed Pat. "He wouldn't know what time o' day it was. He only cares for women and drink. It's that wily Scotsman Deas Thomson who really runs the country. He doesn't want a real row on his hands. He'll back away if we make enough fuss. And we've got friends in Sydney. Dr Lang for one and Henry Parkes for another."

"We must put on as good a front as possible," said Frier, as if enthused by Pat's remarks. "We don't want violence but we've got to make the authorities see we mean business. We got our livings to think of. This is a bread and butter matter for us."

"We'll get a good turnout tomorrow," said Pat. "We've been to all the diggings within five miles of here and the boys have promised to turn out. You can be as constitutional as you like but it will be the show of numbers that'll get us the ten shilling licence."

For an hour the argument swayed one way and the other. Finally it was agreed that four of the leaders, Maxwell, Majoribanks, Frier and Donnelly, would go to the Camp as a deputation from the meeting, then say they were digging without a licence and then see what the Commissioner would do. As Pat pointed out there was no reason to have a meeting and just pass a resolution. The diggers wanted something more positive. And with a couple of thousand angry and armed diggers assembled on Sofala Flat the Commissioner would have to do something or else he was faced with serious trouble. From their knowledge of Mr Green they felt he would have to make some sort of concession to public opinion and it was known that he had the ear of Deas Thomson. At last the meeting broke up and one by one they slipped out into the cool dark night and were off in the direction of their camps.

So on the ninth day of February the sun rose and the day was bright and sunny with a shimmering morning sky that promised heat later on.

The crowd on the Flat gathered around a rough dais made of posts and planks. By eleven o'clock there were almost a thousand people present and every minute more kept trickling in from diggings up and down the river and from distant creeks. Then with the banging of a drum the Mundy Point diggers came marching in all dressed in white moleskins and red shirts, new ribbons on their cabbage tree hats, marching in fours and carrying flags and a great banner that read: "Australia this day expects that every man shall do his duty!" The assembled crowd greeted them with three rousing cheers and noted with approval that most of them carried arms of some sort. Finally when all the diggers were gathered on the Flat and there must have been about two thousand of them the leaders mounted the platform and the elderly Mr Maxwell took the chair and said that the Turon diggers were as loyal as anyone but to submit to the goldfield regulations would be downright degradation. Then the speakers went through the well-known obnoxious clauses of the regulations. And Donnelly said that the object of the regulations was to crush the diggers and drive the bulk of the miners back to the sheep walks of the interior. And the crowd cheered when he said:

"Here we have no masters to order us about and we can work when we like and as we like!"

George was in the crowd with Eliza and he agreed with the sentiments. The Major, of course, was still in hospital and Harry's gentlemanly background prevented him from being associated with such activities. The gold was making the Colony into a proper country, considered George. He was sorry if events moved him so far from his family's opinions but he couldn't abide the Government's policy of oppressing the diggers and there had to be a change. Why shouldn't a fellow go and earn his living in freedom without being badgered by a lot of idlers and parasites? Then it was announced from the dais that in a reply to a previous petition the Colonial Secretary had written that nothing could be done to alter the regulations, particularly the thirty shilling licence. This news was greeted with boos and shouts of protest. The emotion of the crowd was beginning to grew in intensity.

From his window at the Camp Mr Green could hear the shouts and cheers in the valley below. He stood with his hands behind his back biting the ends of his moustache. His assistant commissioners were also in the room now with worried looks upon their faces. His troopers he had ordered to keep to their tents although carrying their arms so they would be ready for action although not provocatively in view. The Camp had already been prepared for defence with firing positions set up. There was a sudden loud cheer from the Flat. Mr Green saw some men detach themselves from the crowd and coming walking up the slope to the Camp. As the men approached he recognised them. Mr Maxwell, Mr Majoribanks, Mr Frier and Mr Donnelly The first two were worthy honest and hardworking diggers who only wanted the wrongs righted. Frier was not a bad fellow, if a bit loud mouthed, while Donnelly, an Irishman, was a bit of a firebrand and the only representative of the physical force boys among the deputation. In the harsh, hot sunlight, their faces deep in shadow under their hats, the four walked slowly up the track to the Camp, came through the entrance and spoke to the trooper on duty at the main door of the Commissioner's office. At the same time the crowd on the Flat moved to the edge of the river and stood in ranks watching the Camp. Even at that distance Mr Green could see that many carried pistols and muskets and those who did not had pick handles and bludgeons.

At that moment the sergeant major came into the room and told Mr Green that parties of diggers were gathered in the hills behind the Camp. This is not the time for rash action, thought Mr Green. It would be best to play a waiting game or else they might find themselves with a little war on their hands which would take more force to control than he had at his disposal at the moment, or perhaps even in the whole Colony. Mr Green asked the sergeant major to bring in the deputation. He greeted them politely and sat them down at his table with the two assistant commissioners standing behind him.

"What can I do for you, gentlemen?" he asked.

Maxwell was the spokesman, a good honest artisan from the West of England who with his own hands had amassed what to him, the son of an English peasant, was a small fortune. He considered it to be highly unjust, a deprivation of his natural rights, that he had to pay taxes without representation, to a government that did nothing for him and in fact hindered his labour. So then began a long argument about the rights and wrongs of the case in which all participated and with Donnelly trying now and again to put in a bit of the physical force view. The talk lasted so long that Mr Green began to feel relieved. He wanted to keep the discussion going as long as possible so the diggers outside would have time to get tired and weary of the whole affair. If their anger was really aroused and they stormed the Camp with their weapons they would make mincemeat of everyone.

Finally the Commissioner said:

"Well, gentlemen, you come here to tell me that you are diggers but have no intention of taking out a licence. Under the law therefore you have committed an offence. I have no option but to bring you before the Sofala Bench of Magistrates to have the matter dealt with."

So Mr Green got up and Drake and Waterford sat down at the table and as magistrates fined the deputation one pound each or two weeks in prison. Mr Green glanced out of the window. There was some shouting and turbulence among the mob of diggers on the Flat and they began to advance across the river and up the slope towards the camp. Mr Green's dark eyes closed to a sliver, his jaws tightened and he put his hand on the hilt of his sword. This was a deuce of a bobbery; he said to himself. We are in for real trouble now! However, several men, among whom he recognised Mr Piddington the little Methodist minister began arguing with the crowd, evidently counselling moderation. The diggers stopped rather unwillingly and milled around for a few minutes. Then a group of three men separated themselves from the crowd and came towards the Camp. Mr Green heaved a sigh of relief. He sent Donald Maclean to tell them that the previous deputation had been fined and was held pending the payment of the fine. The men returned to the Flat and within a few minutes came back with the necessary four pounds. Maxwell and his friends were free! It was no longer possible to apply the gold-field regulations without risking a repetition of the day's events and probably with a less happy ending. Some compromise was needed until the situation changed in favour of the authorities. It suddenly struck Mr Green that almost the safety of the Colony rested on his shoulders. A clash must not take place. There had to be a compromise or rather a concession to the diggers' feelings. He drew a deep breath and said:

"Gentlemen, in view of the events of today I feel that the whole matter of the goldfield regulations should be reconsidered. I intend to bring this to the attention of the Colonial Secretary. In the mean time I intend to reduce the licence fee to half, to fifteen shillings a month, at least for this month, and not apply the other clauses of the regulations which are obnoxious to the diggers until I receive further instructions from Sydney."

Mr Maxwell's face brightened considerably and he warmly shook Mr Green's hand. And when the deputation returned to the crowd of diggers on the Flat a great shout went up. In cheerful mood the diggers assembled in their parties and with flags flying and banners waving, as if for a victory, they marched back to their Points. Here and there they met diggers who had already taken out licences, people who feared the Commissioner and who never took part in protests. Some of the more violent of the diggers broke their cradles and overturned their tents. Otherwise that afternoon there was joy along the river. The diggers went back to work with a will. Now their rights were recognised, and by their own efforts they had made the authorities see reason. The hot sun fell like a red ball to the distant horizon, great white cockatoos with violent yellow crests flew down the valley uttering harsh cries and the ubiquitous kookaburras shouted and screamed ironically from the tops of the river oaks.

CHAPTER 16

At the same moment that Mr Green watched the menacing crowd of diggers gather on Sofala Flat John Murdoch was sitting in Mr Scobe's study in the cleric's home in Glebe. He was there at Mr Scobe's request. The meeting in fact, if John had known, was the result of a plot to return him to the path of righteousness. One evening Mrs McFee had gone to her husband in his study, shut the door and said firmly that something had to be done about young Murdoch. Mr McFee agreed. If the young man's clandestine entanglement with that woman continued he would be too far on the road to perdition to be saved. The outcome was that Mr Scobe was called in and the matter placed before him. He was already aware of the situation. In Sydney everyone was aware of what everyone else did, and news, particularly bad news, travelled fast.

Mr Scobe was a man about fifty to whom the errors and sins of youth and anything that resembled self-indulgence were unknown. The son of a small Protestant farmer in Ulster he had been studious from early youth and his parents pushed him along this path for what future was there in being a small farmer in Ulster, even if of the Protestant faith? And how proud they were when he was ordained! Then he went out to the Australian colonies and by dint of hard work and piety became prominent in the religious life of his community of shopkeepers and merchants, pious clerks and other followers of John Wesley. His life was bounded by church services, prayer meetings, Bible discussions and attempts to counter the lower depths of sin and depravity so characteristic of the Colony. And he was much interested in missionary work in New Zealand and the Islands for if the poor natives were not converted to Christianity and baptised then their souls would not go to Heaven when they came to die.

But sometimes he had great dark fits of depression and when he saw the drunkenness, the debauchery, the destruction of young lives, the hopeless, aimless existence of so many he dared to wonder what God's plan for the world really was. How did God allow the existence of the suppurating sore that was Sydney where people struggled for their daily bread and shelter from the weather often without success? Once returning home he was importuned by a child prostitute and as he rebuffed her a thought from the Bible crossed his mind: "Save thy lambs." He shuddered. Perhaps he was presumptuous in questioning the ways of the Lord. Surely it was not for him to judge? So when the opportunity came of trying to save at least one soul from sin he clutched at it.

Mr Scobe received John in a kindly fashion and said he wished to talk to him about a private matter of utmost importance. He said he knew of John's relationship with a certain woman. He felt his position as a clergyman allowed him to talk frankly about this matter, for he felt that John knew that such a relationship was contrary to the tenets of society and religion. The woman was an outcast who had caught him in her web and if John continued the association he too would be an outcast. One cannot touch pitch without being defiled. On the road to sin there comes a point where there is no return—the path leads inexorably downwards. Should he not stop before it was too late?

John, who had gone to Mr Scobe's home in trepidation, guessed what the interview was to be about and sat in his chair in a state of utmost embarrassment, looking at the design of the carpet. He was a transgressor, he knew, and memories of his boyhood welled up in his mind and the austere and simple life led by his parents, to whom the life he lived with Alice would be beyond comprehension. Mr Scobe said:

"Look at me, John," and John raised his head and was caught by the clergyman's dark eyes that looked piercingly at him from under bushy eyebrows.

"Did not Jesus die for our sake? Have we not been redeemed by the love of God? Tell me, will you ever be able to go to church while you continue to live a life of sin? Will you ever again be able to pray to our Lord without knowing that you have betrayed Him, cast Him out of your life, gone against the guidance He offers you?"

John said nothing but a cold feeling spread through his body and he felt desperate and alone. He suddenly was filled with guilt because he had taken a path that set him aside from his friends, his family and the power of the spirit. Somewhere up above him was a great spiritual force that knew of his every act and who grieved silently because he, John, had strayed from the path.

"Oh," said Mr Scobe, "It is easy to sin, it is easy to take the pleasures of the moment, to live a life of dissipation, despite the fact that this easy path leads to spiritual destruction and often also the destruction of the body."

John's head fell and he again studied the design of the carpet. Mr Scobe's voice reminded him of his father who, when John was a child, often lectured him on some childish transgression, telling him that he had a duty to his father and mother who had brought him into this world of sin. He put his hands over his face and he heard Mr Scobe's voice continue:

"John, you have all your life before you. Perhaps your soul is weary, but you must change your ways and be ashamed of pollution. And you must have strength for moral courage and honour go together. You have many friends who would rejoice to see you take your rightful place in society. Now you are a slave of your desires, but before you. If you can tear yourself from wickedness you will be free."

The clergyman paused and there was a moment's silence.

"Remember God is the goal of every human soul and many paths lead to Him. And night's darkest hour is nearest to the day. You can be forgiven, John, if you do what is lawful and right and turn from wickedness. You shall be forgiven."

John heard Mr Scobe's voice as if it came from a long way off.

"Will, you return to us, John? Will you come back to God and the path of righteousness?"

John's lips trembled and he breathlessly said: "I will."

*   *   *

Mr Scobe realised that for John to break off his relationship with his paramour might be too difficult a task for his new-born resolution, for it was evident that the woman had acquired a strong grip on him. So he suggested that John should return to his home and spend the evening in prayer and he, Mr Scobe, would settle the matter for him. He felt that the woman should be given some monetary assistance to tide her over the immediate separation. John took some notes from his pocket and gave them to the clergyman.

"Give her these," he said, weakly. "Tell her there was no other way."

Mr Scobe conducted John to the front door and shook him firmly by the hand and told him to spend the evening in contemplation of the bright future that lay before him.

"You are now doing what is lawful and right," he said, "And what is acceptable in the eyes of the Lord."

*   *   *

Although Mr Scobe's careful explanation as to John's action

came firstly as a shock, Alice was not really so very surprised. She had felt for some time that her association with him was wilting away, dying from the pressures of his friends and associates.

Mr Scope sat awkwardly in a chair. He had big clumsy feet with heavy black boots and from his peasant father he had inherited big dangling hands more intended by nature to grip a plough or a spade than a prayer book or a Bible.

He told Alice that John Murdoch's friends were concerned about his association with her and had been able to convince him that the path of salvation required that he break off his relationship with Miss King and take a new course. Alice sat opposite Mr Scope, her eyes wide open, her lips slightly parted. She was undoubtedly good to look at and her body although hidden by a simple dress was shapely. Mr Scobe felt a slow blush rise to his face and a feeling of terrible guilt came to him. The bedroom door was slightly open and through it he could see the double bed upon which no doubt John and this comely girl had layen in sinful fornication. He tore his eyes back to Alice and said he hoped that Miss King, too, might take the path of repentance and salvation. It was wished that she should not be left in want and therefore he had for her a sum of money. He placed a small packet on the table.

"Is there any other way in which I can help you?" he asked.

He was suddenly filled with pity for this girl now abandoned in a city full of sin and moral decline. Alice's eyes filled with tears. She shook her head. They both stood up and she held the door wide open and he went out, somewhat shamefaced, his awkward hands dangling uselessly by his side, his face diffused, his eyes hesitant.

Alice shut the door and leaned against it. Men, she thought. There was one who could sooner or later been led into the bedroom. They were all the same, there was only one thing they wanted. She was filled with hatred of men and wanted no more to be concerned with them. The thought of lying with one revolted her. She was filled with hatred and bitterness.

Nevertheless she remembered there was only one thing about her relationship with John and that was it had taken her away from College Street. He had taken her away for his own reasons, of course, so he could have her to himself for his own pleasure. But when his pleasures were satisfied and social pressures were put upon him then he abandoned her, the weak creature that he was. She cried a little then blew her nose and wiped her eyes. She was lonely and frightened and wondered what lay before her. She looked out the window. Sydney was a wilderness, a place full of indifferent people. What was she to do? Remain at Miss M'Cackie's and work from morn till dusk? Miss M'Cackie was a slave driver to her half dozen seamstresses, the hours were long and the pay miserable. What else to do? Go back to Madam Rose? That was unthinkable. She thought of her sister Eliza, gone away to the wild goldfields, somewhere in the endless forests of the interior, far from the dubious civilisation of Sydney town. Then she remembered that John Murdoch had been there. There must be a coach that went all the way, just as in England; and surely it would be possible for a lone woman to go there? It would be an arduous and even dangerous journey but she ached to see Eliza again, to be with someone she loved, instead of being among indifferent strangers.

*   *   *

The coach journey up to the West proved to be an event unlike any which Alice had previously experienced. It was the first time she had been in a four wheel vehicle and the first time she had been out of the dusty streets of Sydney. The coach proved to be a rough box on wheels drawn by four horses with seats inside and some on the roof for hardy travellers prepared to endure the sun, the heat and the dust, or the rain, according to the weather. Inside with Alice were a couple of commercial gentlemen, with a squatter and his wife who were taking a new governess back to their station. On the roof were a trio of down-cast diggers returning from a spree in Sydney. Alice paid her fare all the way to Sofala. This was seven pounds, a lot of money, and she was not surprised that poor people travelled all the way to the goldfields on foot. For endless hours the coach bumped, rattled and jerked its way over the rough road, stopping now and then to change horses and give the diggers a chance to revive their spirits with a noggin or two. The road wound on and on, over plains, up great mountains, down precipitous tracks where it seemed that coach and passengers might at any moment be flung into the abyss. The narrow, rutted, dusty road was the umbilical cord that connected the rich inland of wool and gold to the shabby port from whence ships took the Colony's wealth all the way to distant England. It was busy with diggers walking to the goldfields, wool drays on the way to Sydney, loads of goods going up the country. At last the coach broke out of the dense bush into the wide Bathurst plains lying peacefully quiet under the vast dome of the blue sky. As the afternoon ended the coach rattled through Kelso, splashed over the river, up the far bank with a rush and soon drew up before Mr Rotton's hotel. Alice was still relatively well off, with seventeen pounds left from John Murdoch's money and several pounds of her own, so she took a room for the night to rest her weary bones before setting off for Sofala in the coach at eight o'clock next morning.

*   *   *

Next morning the coach started off on time along the rough Sofala track, just a line drawn across the country without any shaping or grading, full of potholes and ruts. Alice began to take more heed of the landscape; the dry rolling plains, the tree-lined creeks, the crowds of native birds that rose in the air and screeched as the coach passed by, the cloudless blue sky, the herds of cattle, the flocks of sheep, the rough dwellings, the cool morning breeze on her cheek. What lay ahead of her, she wondered? Was Eliza still at the goldfields, or would Alice arrive in some rough town, friendless and alone; what did the future hold? At Peel the horses were changed and the men went into the inn in search of the inevitable noggin. When the coach reached Wyagdon's towering wall all the men got off and walked while the coach was hauled by the panting horses to the summit. Here they rested a while and Alice dozed off in her corner seat.

*   *   *

She was suddenly awakened by the coach jerking to a halt, by shouts, a scream from the plump woman opposite her, gruff commands. She looked out of the window. There were three men standing by the coach, with guns in their hands.

"All of you out," shouted one. "Quickly now!"

The passengers struggled down and stood in a line with their backs against the coach. There were two women travelling as well as Alice; one plump and well-dressed, accompanied by her husband who gave the appearance of prosperity. The other was a gaunt elderly woman in dark clothes. Of the four men travelling outside three looked like diggers and the fourth a frightened looking clerk or shopman. Alice descended from the coach and stood with the others, her heart beating with fear. These, then, were the terrible bushrangers spoken of in Sydney with bated breath. She looked at the men. One, obviously in command, was big and brutal with hard eyes and a slit mouth. He carried a gun and there were two pistols and a knife in his belt. The second was an older man with a grey and bitter face, and the third was a lad, but as fierce-looking as the others. They all had the same look, the same stance, the same bitter eyes. "Vandemonians!" whispered the plump woman in terror.

The Vandemonians acted with efficient haste. While the elder two pointed their weapons at the prisoners the younger one went from one to the other taking watches, rings, pocketbooks and any valuables he could lay his hands on. He wrenched open Alice's bag and took out her purse and held aloft in triumph her remaining money. When the search was complete and the booty was gathered up, scarcely five minutes had passed. The leader's eyes rested on Alice for a moment.

"We'll take the girl," he cried and jerked her away from the other passengers by the arm.

"Youse stay here," he called. "Follow us and we'll blow your heads off."

The passengers stood in the bright sunlight as if stunned. Alice, her arm held in a fierce grip by her captor, found herself whirled off into the thick bush by the side of the road. For five minutes they careered through the bush and then halted. They stood for a moment, breathing heavily. Then the leader of the bushrangers said to his mates:

"Youse go on, I'll catch up with you at the camp."

He stood holding Alice's arm while his mates disappeared down the track, the younger with a sly grin on his face. When they were alone the man pressed Alice against his hot, smelly body and looked at her with his cruel eyes.

"Youse know what I want, don't youse," he said.

Alice suddenly lost her fear and was filled with angry resentment. She began to struggle; she hated this vile creature who was bent on destroying her. Too long had she been abused by men.

"Youse do what's er told," he cried. "I'll teach you what's what!"

She struggled even more violently and as she fought against him her hand fell upon the haft of the knife he carried.in his belt. She slipped it from its sheath and dodging under his arm plunged it firmly in his belly.

The man who a moment ago had been so strong and urgent in his wishes suddenly stood stock still. Alice sprang back from him. With.an effort he pulled out the knife of which about four inches had penetrated his body and dropped it on the ground.

He stood with his mouth slightly open, his eyes looking in a puzzled and almost pitiful way at Alice. Blood gushed from the wound and flowed in a stream down his trousers. His face turned an ashen grey and he slumped slowly to the ground, his back against a tree. Alice hesitated; what to do next? She felt no remorse, no pity for the man. Then it came to her that if her attacker's mates came back they would make short work of her. She turned to go. The man on the ground called to her in a thin voice:

"Help me, help me. Don't leave me here alone."

But she ran off through the bush, stumbling through the thick undergrowth until, out of breath, she collapsed in a clearing among the trees.

*　　*　　*

It was nearing midday when the coach was held up and it was late in the afternoon when Alice came to herself again and the shadows were beginning to lengthen. She struggled to her feet, holding to a tree for support. She was parched with thirst and hungry. The green bush surrounded her entirely. There was not a sound to be heard except for the occasional twittering of unseen birds. She was lonely but not frightened. Which way should she go? She looked around her. There were no paths, so sign of human habitation, nothing but the endless grey green leaves, trees that towered up to the sky, thick brush that covered the ground. She supposed she had to go somewhere. There was no point in staying where she was and she might still be within reach of the sinister Vandemonians perhaps eager to avenge their mate. So she stumbled through the undergrowth, pushing branches aside, climbing over fallen trees. She came to a little trickle of a creek where she was able to drink and wipe her face and hands. Once as she entered a small clearing something big and grey bounced off from under her feet and she screamed and clasped her hands to her mouth It came to her that this must be one of the Colony's strange animals, the kangaroo that hopped on its back legs. Then a little while later she came to another clearing and there, on a boulder in the sun sat a big lizard like creature with a darting tongue that looked at her with a cool stare. Alice froze, her heart pounding with fear. The creature flicked its tongue once more, gave her sardonic look and scrabbled off into the undergrowth.

Night was beginning to fall and the air turned cooler. She was well and truly lost in the bush. There must be some human habitation somewhere and footsore as she was there was no alternative but to look for it. Weary, she paused for a moment. Then some way off she caught the glimmer of a light, a faint flickering light. She turned in its direction and struggled through the dark towards it. After a few minutes of effort she came near enough to see a camp fire, the outline of a tent and two men seated by the fire. Hope swelled in her heart and she called out. Thee two men turned towards her. Then she reached an open space and ran across it towards the fire.

"I'm lost, I'm lost," she cried.

The bigger of the two men rose to his feet and in the light of the fire she could see that he was an enormous black man with a crown of white hair.

*   *   *

That was the second time that Alice fainted that day. When she recovered she was lying on a heap of blankets. The bigger of the two black men was sitting beside her and gave her a pannikin of water to sip as soon as she could sit up. He was an African, she knew, not an Aborigine. He spoke to her in English as good as her own and gave her some food.

"Now you go to sleep," he said. "Tomorrow we'll take you where you want to go."

It turned out next morning that they were indeed Africans and had lived long in England and that was why they spoke the language so well. They had been some time at the diggings and finding the alluvial claims too overcrowded they came up the hills to sink a shaft, thinking that the mother lode of the gold washed into the creeks by time might be here. Alice told them what had happened to her and they were indeed shocked and complained that the troopers were too busy chasing the diggers to clear out the bushrangers and other criminals attracted to the diggings to prey on the diggers. They asked her where she was going and she said she was looking for her sister who was working somewhere on the Turon, perhaps in a hotel.

"And what's her name?" asked the elder of the two. Alice told him.

"Isn't she the girl who cooks for George Barton's party down at Green Point?" said the younger one in his deep voice.

"She would be nearly sixteen by now," said Alice.
"That's right and her name's Eliza."

After some breakfast the younger man took her through the bush and down into a steep valley.

"Look," he said. "Do you see that tent by the river's edge. That's what you are looking for."

No one was more surprised five minutes later than Eliza to see her sister walking towards her.

CHAPTER 17

One afternoon the inhabitants of Sofala and the diggers working on the river claims near the town were astonished to catch a glimpse of red coats among the trees and the glint of sunshine on steel. Then on the long hill coming down into the town marched a detachment of troops, dusty and sunburnt, but marching firmly and with fixed bayonets. At the head of the column rode an officer and at the rear two wagons carried the men's gear. The people came out of the houses and tents and some of the diggers scrambled up from the river flats to watch the troops march past. The soldiers' heavy tramp echoed through the streets as they passed the flimsy houses, the tawdry hotels and the garish shops. At the ford they turned right and crossed the river, splashing through the narrow stream, and marched up the hill to the Camp. There a guard turned out and presented arms. Behind the guard were ranged the fifty mounted troopers Mr Green managed to collect all armed with sabre and carbine, in the style of the Irish Constabulary, a body which had proved so very successful in keeping order in that country, as Mr Green once remarked.

That evening there was consternation among the diggers. Mr Green's mangy troopers were one thing but forty men of the Eleventh Regiment were very much another. Tall athletic fellows bronzed and fit from their one hundred and sixty mile march from Sydney, smart, well trained and determined, they would be in fire power more than a match for the diggers. The Sofala people with irony nicknamed the soldiers the Army of Occupation of the Turon . Now things didn't look so good and in the next few days the stream of diggers going to Port Phillip increased and the road to Bathurst was crowded with parties going south.

Those who remained were both angry and despondent. They

began to feel that they had been deceived by the Commissioner. They walked up the hill to the Camp and looked at the red-coats peacefully washing their shirts, polishing their boots and cleaning their muskets. Then the diggers walked down the hill again hands in pockets sucking their black pipes or pulling their beards and scowling at the white cockatoos that flew shrieking overhead. A few more days passed, a few more diggers went off to Victoria and a few more troopers arrived to reinforce the Camp. Then one morning out came a little procession from the Camp. It was headed by Mr Waterford on horseback followed by a dozen mounted troopers and an equal number of foot police. Down they went to the river and along the claims in the shadow of Lucky Point. Here and there Mr Waterford reined in his horse by a claim and called out to the owner:

"Hey, you, my man, where's your licence?"

All the while the troopers sat sternly on their horses, their hands on the pommels of their sabres while the grim foot police watched with their carbines slung upon their shoulders. Most diggers, of course, could not produce a licence and in a short time a dozen men surrounded by police were marched back to the Camp. As they walked in the gate the half company was on parade practicing musket drill, fixing and unfixing bayonets as if to show to all the high level of their efficiency. And the twelve diggers were taken one by one before the Sofala bench of magistrates and fined a pound each and told that if they wanted to continue to dig for gold they would have to pay for a licence which, thanks to the good graces of Mr Green would this month only cost them fifteen shillings.

Was there consternation! Even more were they enraged and dismayed when the next day Mr Drake came out and took not twelve but twenty diggers and conveyed them back to the Camp to go before the magistrates and be fined. Then each day onwards the troopers rode out of the camp, bringing back twenty or thirty disconsolate diggers until all the likely places within reach were visited. There were violent disagreements among the diggers. The physical force boys called for strong action and resistance. But when they were approached by the troopers their resistance collapsed and they would be led off like lambs to the Camp. So there were reproaches and quarrels and more people went off to Victoria in disgust. Times were hard, too, because of the water shortage and the sickness that ensued. To the few diggers still doing well the fine and the licence fee were to be tolerated. But for the majority it meant hardship and for those who by backbreaking work might only be getting an ounce or two a week to keep a family at goldfield prices the situation mean abject poverty and absolute misery. So when February came to an end and it was the first day of March, most diggers went to take out a licence. But the canny Mr Green realising that he controlled the situation now demanded the full thirty shillings. He ignored the sullen looks of the diggers for he knew that as long as he had the forty redcoats and forty muskets and bayonets in the Camp he was safe. And Mr Deas Thomson told him to keep the troops as long as he liked. The situation anyhow for the moment was safely in hand. George and the rest of the party at Green Point accepted life as it came and paid the licence fee, grumbling. What else to do? Perhaps they should have gone to Victoria? But tales were coming back to the Turon that the situation there was no better and the goldfields police and the commissioners even more arrogant than in New South Wales.

It was a bit of a surprise for the diggers at Green Point when Eliza's grown up sister joined the George Barton Party. The tale soon spread of how she had been in a coach held up by bushrangers and was saved by Uncle Tom and his friend, the two Africans. However, George and his party were looked upon as respectable people and not likely to behave in a way that such stern Methodists such as Mr Treganza and his friends would disapprove of. After a while Alice's presence was taken for granted;

anyhow she worked hard around the camp, even helping with the cradle, and the diggers always respected hard workers. But it was Alice who was surprised when at last the Major came back from hospital, pale and thin, clumsy on his new crutches. He complained about being unsteady on his pins but Dr Johnstone assured him that when his stump was well enough to take a timber leg he would be as agile as ever.

The moment Alice saw the Major the memories came flooding back. When she had not been long on the streets, and only just fifteen, she met the Major one evening in the Haymarket. Then for a year or more she went once or twice a week to his rooms. He took a bit of a fancy to her and she did not find him disagreeable. In those days he was a handsome man, well set up and self possessed, the epitome of a gentleman. When Alice became ill she saw no more of him and when at last she went address she found he had gone away. How he had changed! He was now a poor broken man who sat beside the fire for long periods and looked into its red mysterious depth. He had little to say to Alice but it was obvious that you don't go to bed with a woman a couple of times a week for a year or more without remembering what she looks like. Then he had been the master; now he was a poor fellow helped by his mates While Alice, once a woman he paid to go to bed with him, was an equal partner in a common enterprise.

*   *   *

Anyhow the last heap of dirt from the Green Point claim was washed in what seemed to be the last pailful of water from the Turon's drought stricken trickle. Now it was time to move to the new claim at Heath's Point which George had already pegged and registered with the Commissioner's office. So a hired dray came and on it were piled the tent, the tools, the cradle and various bits of timber they salvaged from the shaft and the long tom, and took themselves off to the new location. Once they settled in, the tent erected, the cooking fire going, with Eliza making the dinner, George thought he would make a trip to Bathurst. He had money to pay into the Bank, including some of the Major's and Harry's, to be put away before they wasted it on drink and gambling. Pat was off to his father's place to lie low for a while and to George he entrusted money to be put away for a rainy day. Also, George's old horse Polly was eating her head off in Mr Lewis' paddock and he intended to ride her back to the Turon. One morning therefore George awoke early, long before dawn, and set off -up a back creek that led towards Wattle Flat. The birds were not even astir as he tramped through the quiet bush and bright-eyed possums watched him from the trees and a grazing wallaby bounced away from under his feet. The Wattle Flat diggers were still asleep as he passed through the collection of ragged tents and bark humpies that marked the village. The sun rose as he reached the top of the Wyagdon escarpment, the rays glistening over the black and menacing heights of Mount Horrible away to the east and illuminated the endless miles of bush covered hills and valleys to the westward.

George filled his lungs with the crystal fresh air. Ah, despite the troubles and the hardships all the problems of the Turon, the licence, the drought and so. on, it was good to be alive and to be part of the great gold rush that was transforming the country. The months since he left Goonigal were rich and varied in experience, His old life seemed far away, like a dream of long ago, not quite real. He shook his head, smiled to himself and strode down the steep Wyagdon track. At the inn at the bottom of the track he stopped for a rest, a pint of Colonial ale, a slice of damper with some cheese made in Bathurst at Mr Dakin's property.

*   *   *

In Bathurst George called at his brother-in-law's place and gave him the money to put in the Bank, where it would be safe. Mr

Lewis urged him to go to Sydney where Rolly and his family were still on holiday. But no, he would stay in Bathurst for a few days only because there was work waiting for him on the Turon. However, he made himself popular with his sister Ann for he gave her a handful of nuggets wherewith to have made a brooch and a ring for herself. She smiled at him. He was her youngest brother, they had played together as children. Once, she remembered, when he was only seven or eight they were bailed up in a paddock by a wall-eyed bullock who made menacing movements at them. Little George fronted up bravely at the beast and beat it off with a stick.

"George, dear," she said. "The family think you ought to give up this gold digging business. Father would like you back at Goonigal. You know he's old and far from well."

"I know, Annie," George replied. "Perhaps I ought to go and see the old man, but I'm busy and people depend on me."

She said no more on the subject but asked him about his companions.

"Henry mentioned you have a girl to do the cooking," she said.

"Oh, Eliza! Yes, she's really good, looks after us like a mother and works night and day." Then he told her something of Eliza's history, and also that he sister, who had a hard time in Sydney, was now with them.

"And how old is Eliza?"

"Oh, coming up sixteen, I suppose."

It was not that Ann was unkind but she was wiser in the ways of the world than George. She knew that when a girl was rising sixteen and she was thrown together with a young man such as George in the free atmosphere of the diggings it made a dangerous and inflammable mixture. She knew her George only too well. As likely or not he'd end by marrying the girl. He has, she thought, none of the sense of the distinction of social position that a person of his background ought to have. However, Ann finally persuaded her brother to made a visit to Goonigal and see his father, on the grounds that Mr Barton was in bad health, so bad in fact that the doctor doubted whether he would live beyond the year's end. The truth was that George was never very close to his father. In the first ten or fifteen years at Goonigal Mr Barton was so busy dealing with floods, droughts, fires, the scab and the other plagues of the squatter that he had little time for his children except to scold them if they got under his feet.

It was not until later years, especially when his health began to fail, that the old man began to warm towards his last born. Nevertheless the two felt awkward in each other's company. So when George arrived at Goonigal after two days hard riding on old Polly unused to such exercise father and son sat on the veranda, drinking black tea and talking in monosyllables while watching a mob of white cockatoos in a stand of timber down by the creek. The old place was much changed since George went away. Most of the men were gone to the diggings and only Joseph remained and he was now failing. There were a couple of raw lads hired from somewhere, too unadventurous to go after gold. Also Rolly had hired from Captain Towns four Chinese coolies He paid the Captain eight pounds each for them and the coolies were under contract to work for him for five years at three shillings a week — a much more reasonable remuneration than the outrageous wages demanded by white labour. However the coolies proved to be neither as hardworking nor as docile as expected and there was a fear that they might take off for the diggings to look for gold.

However, George didn't like it. Goonigal was no longer the old place where everyone worked together. The white workers didn't like the Chinese and the Chinese — well, no one knew what they liked or disliked. There was ill feeling all around.

After a couple of days George felt he'd had enough of the place, it was too gloomy and depressing. He told his father he had to be on the way back to the diggings and promised half-heartedly to return , probably at Christmas. As he said it he knew he was telling a lie, that he really had no intention of coming back. The old man was embarrassed and waved sadly from the veranda as George rode off. It was a sad parting for both. Polly ambled along the track, then they crossed the river and left the flat country behind them. Along the way the country was green and well watered with plenty of feed on it. Just the place for a sheep property, thought George. You would never go short of water even in a dry season. But he was low in spirit, even stopping at a wayside shanty for a noggin and a yarn with a couple of diggers trying their luck in the nearby river didn't manage to cheer him up. He felt he had seen his father for the last time and perhaps the old home too, the place where his youth was spent. It was evident that Rolly and Amelia and even his father now saw him on the other side of the fence, on the diggers' side. Or was it his fault, and by going to the diggings had rejected his family?

He remembered Amelia's remark about "ruffians and republicans." Why, he knew well from experience, from living among them, that the diggers were good fellows who worked hard and were always ready to help a mate. True, they would not fit comfortably into Amelia's drawing room. But both Rolly and Amelia were foolish. They put up a high wall between themselves and the rest of the world. They didn't understand that the diggers were making the country rich. But where did the future lie? Certainly not for George going back to Goonigal. He would not be able to put up with it after the freedom of the diggings. No, there was plenty of alluvial gold in the Colony. He would stick to the diggers and the diggings and perhaps make his fortune after all.

And what about his mates? More important what about Eliza? There was already almost an understanding between them. It was customary now for Eliza and he to talk things over and then George would go to the others and say: "Don't you think we should do this or that?" As he jogged towards Bathurst it suddenly struck him that his relationship with Eliza was very close, almost like man and wife, except that they did not share the same bed. And now that she was growing into such a handsome girl sooner or later it would come to that. And he would marry her. All his digger mates would expect this as a right and proper thing. Of course, he considered, this would mean a complete break with his family. His sister Annie was kind enough but he could already see the look on Amelia's face. "Who is this girl?" she would say. If George married some simpering little thing with pretentions to gentility she would be accepted. But loyal, hardworking Eliza, never! He would not tolerate Eliza being insulted so a marriage would mean breaking with his family and going away, perhaps to Victoria. He suddenly realised that he took it for granted that he and Eliza would be married. Would she have him? He knew she would. Ever since he pulled her out of the river he knew she would.

* * *

When at last George arrived back among the dusty red brick houses of Bathurst he felt more cheerful. He was, in some ways, a changed man since he left Goonigal. The old life was well and truly behind him, the old narrow life in which everyone had a place, like letters in pigeon holes, confined, boring. Now the world stretched before him, for him to do with as he would and the old life no longer had a hold over him.

The Bathurst streets were crowded, the lights were bright, the shops and bars were busy. George walked around the town and met with a couple of diggers he knew and they had a quiet drink at the Royal Hotel. But the peace was broken by a quarrel between some Irishmen and two Orangemen over some nonsense about the battle of the Boyne, wherever that was. Like most of the native born George found this disputes incomprehensible.

He tried to calm the contestants but one of the Orangemen took a set at him and called him a disloyal mick. George told him not to be stupid and the man aimed a blow which grazed his cheek. George caught him in a vice like grip and threw the fellow on the floor which shook him so much he crawled away. George couldn't stand fools, no road.

It was extraordinary how ill tempered the diggers became after their defeat at the hands of Mr Green. Everyone was cantankerous and angry, ready for dispute. Each night at Sofala there were fights between the Irish and the Cornish or Orangemen. Then there came stories of trouble on the Meroo where a hundred of Chinese had gathered to dig for gold and Mr Green sent troopers to protect the Celestials. The diggers disliked the Chinese because they were squatters' cheap labour and now were taking gold that rightly belonged to the diggers. When Mr Green sent his troopers to protect the Chinese this merely confirmed the digger opinion that the squatters wanted the Chinese to win as much gold as possible so it would run out and the diggers would have to go back to shepherding. Among most of the Sofala diggers there was a spirit of disillusionment and ill humour. People were downcast and unhappy. Now it was all hard work and little gain. The merchants who set up well-stocked shops in Bathurst to supply the goldfields were disconsolate as they watched the diggers troop off in the direction of Port Phillip.

The men in flash suits with shiny hats on the back of their heads who dealt in claims and leases now sat in bar rooms their hands in their pockets, saying that the cream was skimmed off the New South Wales diggings and they were just settling their affairs before going off themselves to Ballarat or Bendigo.

George stayed on a few more days in Bathurst with his sister and ambled around the shops to see if there was anything he needed to buy. In one shop he saw a pile of books and looking through them a titled caught his eye: Principles of Geology, by

Charles Lyell. This was something he ought to know more about so he purchased it for reading in the candle light in the tent on the evenings. He took it home and showed it to his sister and there was a clergyman there, Mr Melville, a curate of the English church, who told him that it was a bad book, that Lyell's principle of uniformitarianism was unacceptable and contrary to the tenets of religion and morality. Besides, had not Bishop Heber said that the world was created by God only some six thousand years ago, which he had deduced by his study of the Bible?

George shook his head with wonder that a man should know so much, but nevertheless put the book aside for future reading.

CHAPTER 18

For Alice the first days at Green Point were like emerging from a long dark tunnel into the light of day. Or waking from a bad dream. Her past was now behind her and she felt she had left it as a snake sloughs off an old skin. When she awoke in the morning the sunlight was so pure, the air so clear, the present so vivid and the past now so misted over. There was work to be done, food to be prepared, people to be looked after. She began by helping Eliza with the cooking but there was not work enough for two so she sometimes helped the men at the claim, usually working the cradle when there was enough water to wash with. No one asked how she had lived in Sydney and why she had so suddenly appeared on the Turon. This was very much the attitude of the goldfields. People were judged not by what they had been but what they were at the moment. Your mates might have been labourers, convicts, barristers, landed gentry or pickpockets or farmers. What was important was how well they worked and whether they were good mates or not, which meant a respect for common property and the ability to stand by you in time of trouble. To the diggers, therefore, the past was a closed book and often for good reason.

When Alice and Eliza were left alone with the Major and Harry Pole during George's trip to Bathurst and Goonigal they found these two became more conversational. But they tended to talk to each other and fell back on the sort of conversation used by people of their class. Their attitude to the girls was fraternal enough nevertheless. They kept at a distance for they were not always quite sure how to treat women who were not of their own class.

In the past they had associated with women of two kinds — their mothers, sisters, cousins, the wives and female relations, of their friends whom they treated with respect and as social equals. The other types of women were the servants or the prostitutes. The older female servants they ignored except to order them to bring tea or hot water or a clean towel. The younger servants they pawed when they got them alone and sometime: succeeded in pushing them over on the bed. The girls often acquiesced in this, sometimes because they were flattered by the attention and anyhow they were brought up to believe that if the master wanted something he had to have it. Prostitutes of course were women one passed an occasional half hour with and little conversation was required. And anyhow both servants and prostitutes were on the same level, women of an inferior social class who existed for the pleasure and comfort of the masters. With Eliza it was different. True she came from an inferior grade of society yet they both treated her and her sister politely not only because it would have caused George's displeasure if they had done otherwise but because of the very nature of the relationship. They were partners in a common project and it didn't matter whether you had been to Eton or had spent a couple of years in a dame school. What was important was the way you behaved. In fact on occasions Eliza scolded both the Major and Harry Pole for the way they kept their things; Like most people accustomed to being waited on they were untidy when they had to fend for themselves. So the relationship was a sort of division of labour and it never entered into the men's head to be anything but polite and respectful and to be guided by Eliza in all the things that came within her sphere. Alice, however, was a slightly different case. Harry sometimes looked at her longingly although she treated him rather as if he was a little boy. The Major was different. From the look in his eyes Alice knew he remembered her. But how different he was now, this poor, one-legged man, with a lined face and haunted eyes. How handsome he had been, walking down the Haymarket with a military swagger, his shiny top hat, his silver mounted cane in one hand, his elegant gloves in the other. Some of the girls would have been ready to go with him for nothing. So of an evening they would sit around the fire, Eliza and Alice not saying a word, while the two men chatted to each other of the past.

Harry would talk about England, about his parent's home in Dorset, riding to hounds, shooting over covets, or about Eton or the people he knew at Oxford; As the conversation developed they would gradually forget they were only rough diggers on the Turon in a far-distant Colony and slip back into their previous status and the Major would say

"By Jove, Harry, once I lost a couple of ponies at White's. The fellows there play for deuced high stakes and I've seen thousands won and lost in a night."

And Harry would say:

"When I was at Eton I knew a fellow, Gatsby was his name, who was later in your regiment."

And the Major would say:

"Did you ever know the Brooks, who owned Brookscotes, about ten miles from your parents' place?"

Then some rough digger would emerge into the firelight and bring both of them back to earth by saying:

"'As youse coves seen me 'orse wot got lost this mornin' and might be over this way?"

And the Major would reply in the vernacular:

"No, mate, we 'aven't seen so 'orse 'ere."

And the fellow would nod his thanks and disappear again into the darkness. And while Eliza poured out another pannikin of black tea the two men would fall silent and look into the dying embers of the fire, wondering what fate had in store for them.

One evening Harry said his ambition was to make a lot of money at the diggings and go back to England in style where his family would be happy to see him again. At this the Major said nothing for he knew that he could never go back because he would never be welcome and sooner or later people would start asking awkward questions about money. His parents were dead and his brothers and sister and their families considered him to be dead too, and disgraced and his name never more to be spoken of. Eliza looked at Harry with her shrewd little eyes for she knew all about the price of money and had known it since she could walk. She thought he was a poor simple fellow for all that he had been at Eton. He would never make money for he could never keep a penny in his pocket for long and the fact that he had a few pounds in the bank was because he was George's partner.

In George's absence Harry Pole and the Major set to work on the claim. Harry sunk a shaft and the Major helped him set up a windlass. The Major was handy enough at hauling up buckets from the shaft or working the cradle. But with a pick and shovel he was hopeless. His wooden leg would slip in the dirt and stones and he couldn't keep his balance. When no one was looking he would practice but it took him half an hour to move the amount of dirt a complete man would shift in five minutes. It was pathetic Eliza thought when she saw him once throw his shovel away in a rage and press his fists against his eyes. When he took his hands away they were wet. Eliza pretended not to notice but she nevertheless felt how strange it was that a real gentleman like the ones she used to see walking down the Haymarket in frock coats and top hats with silver mounted canes should be found digging on a heap of gravel wearing rough clothes and weeping because he could no longer work with a pick and shovel like some common working man.

Nevertheless the claim progressed apace and soon Harry had

the shaft down ten feet and the Major would take the cradle to the river's edge and wash a bit of dirt. There was no point in putting in a long tom for there was not sufficient water in the river. Even with Alice helping with the cradle they only obtained an ounce or two a week, hardly wages.

There was still discontent and unhappiness among the diggers on the Turon as the scorching summer turned to a more gentle autumn. People were jumpy and nervy, too, ready to abandon a good claim and go off on some wild goose chase. A digger could come to Sofala and say that a mob was getting twenty ounces a day each somewhere or other and in a flash people would pack up their belongings and with a cradle perched on their shoulders march off to some distant and lonely creek. There was a sudden rush to Palmers' Oakey and in a few days there were five hundred diggers there, and parties hurried off to greener pastures and hopefully to golden holes at Jew's Mountain, Tambaroora Greek or the Dirt Holes. The weather was still hot but heavy black clouds began to gather. This went on for days but not a drop of rain. The diggers all wanted rain, as long as it didn't flood.

*   *   *

George, back from Bathurst, set to work on the claim. If this one was as good as Green Point they still might make a fortune. But there was no water in the river worth worrying about, scarcely enough to drink and cook with, so they gave up working the cradle and piled the dirt up in a great heap near the shaft, to be washed later when there was water. With George's help the shaft was put down twenty feet when the false bottom was reached — as hard as iron. So George once again went into Sofala and bought some black powder and safety fuse and at the end of the day's work set off a blast, causing all the bird life of Heath's Point to circle madly in the air chattering and cawing. That evening with the smell of gunpowder still in their nostrils they sat down to the evening meal surrounded by the black night where here and there campfires twinkled like jewels. Then a few spots of rain hissed into the fire. Rain! At last and it would make the river flow again and clear out the revolting filth accumulated in its bed since the drought began. They went off to bed with the sound of gentle rain on the canvas roof of the tent. But scarcely had they been asleep an hour when they were awoken by a wild, roaring gale.

Harry lit a lantern and then Alice and Eliza appeared as their little tent at the back of the big one was blown down and they were soaked to the skin. Rover crawled in, too, his tail between his legs and found himself a dry spot under one of the stretchers. They dozed through the dismal night and then came the even more dismal dawn. The river, almost non-existent the previous evening, now spread from bank to bank, a wide expanse of madly flowing yellow water. The hundred yards width of river gravel dotted with claims was now many feet under the roaring mass of water which bore rapidly downstream uprooted trees, planks and boxes, the occasional cradle, a dead sheep or steer and once even the body of a drowned digger rolling over and over in the flood. The river kept a steady roaring noise that never stopped day or night and was echoed back from the high whinstone crags. The three men and the two girls sat in the dismal dark tent knowing that all the work of the last weeks was gone for nothing. The shaft was now filled with mud, the heap of gold bearing dirt ready to put through the cradle was washed miles down the river along with the cradle, the windlass, the picks and the shovels. For three days it rained without stopping and the river rose over the banks and began to creep up the hill so fast that the tent had to be moved for fear of inundation. For a week more there were heavy showers every day. Finally the downpour ceased. But all was soaked. The tent and the bedding, clothing, firewood and the ground itself, which oozed water at every footstep. Every tree dripped water from its leaves and the diggers sat in the tents, coats and collars up round their necks, depressed and angry, cursing their fate. The whole country for miles around was soaked with water. Every tributary of the Turon was filled and every little creek sent a regular stream of muddy water to swell the raging flow of the river. People scarcely moved from their tents. It was impossible to go far for every creek was up and the tracks were deep in mud. A few brave ones went out to look for dry firewood or to tramp through mud to the knees to buy food or more important a black square bottle of rum with which to keep away the cold and the fevers.

And what desolation and misery the flood brought to the diggers! For those who did well or even fairly well they had money to fall back on if they hadn't spent it on drink and gambling, but for the seven tenths of the diggers who just made wages and even in the best of times had a hard struggle to survive it was a disaster. And the fevers and the rheumatisms and the agues made the doctors busy along the river.

"The floods mean disappointment, sickness, hope deferred, hard living and in some cases absolute misery not only for the diggers but for their wives and children," said Dr Johnson one day as he called in passing to see how the Major was progressing with his wooden leg. It would be weeks before the riverbed would be dry enough to work again, so George suggested that they abandon their claim and take up a dry claim at Wattle Flat. He'd been told that Uncle Tom's Hill by the top of Big Oakey Creek was a favoured position. They would have to buy a cart to take the dirt down to the river for washing. First they would shift camp, start work on the new claim and hope that it paid. But this was the digger's life — prosperity for a while for the lucky ones followed by hard work and the chance of poverty for many.

Since quite early in the history of the Turon field people had worked at Green Wattle Flat or just Wattle Flat as it later became known. There was a fair success but nothing spectacular, not like some of the rich bed claims on the Turon. Then the two Africans who had helped Alice sunk a shaft in a hill to the east of Big Oakey Creek and found a real golden hole. As one of them had a thatch of white hair the locality became known as Uncle Tom's Hill. But my word, as George said, it was difficult work there. The ground was hard and often had to be blasted with black powder which put up the cost of sinking and you had to go down fifty or sixty feet to find a stratum of washing stuff. This however was about four feet thick and easily cradled. But it had to be hauled to the surface all of sixty feet, loaded on the cart and driven to the river for cradling. Slow, hard and arduous work but rewarding for one day they found thirty ounces in the clean up and most days not much less. Soon there was a crowd on the hill and George could count as many as eighty odd claims of which over thirty were doing well.

One morning George was working underground timbering part of the drive where the ground was poor. Since the Major lost his leg George had become very careful and cautious. He would tap the walls and the back of the drive with a hammer and listen carefully to be sure the rock was solid and check that the timber was firmly chocked in place. The drive followed a layer of wash dirt downhill. How long would it last, how soon would it pinch out? These were the questions George kept asking himself. By now he was a pretty good practical miner. Nothing like as good as Treganza and his friends but nevertheless knowing about the lie of the land and where gold was most likely to be found, that slate was an indicator and that quartz stained with ironstone showed promising ground.

A voice boomed down the shaft. It was Harry calling him.

George scrambled to the bottom of the shaft. The Commissioner wished to see him, Harry said. So George put his foot in the loop at the end of the rope and Harry slowly winched him to the surface. There stood Mr Green in his smart uniform with a couple of troopers and two young gentlemen, slim, elegant, with interested and enquiring faces. The Commissioner greeted George and said to his two companions:

"Gentlemen, may I introduce to you Mr George Barton, one of our successful diggers. Mr Barton is native born and his father is a gentleman settler who came to the Colony many years ago."

He turned to George and said:

"Mr Barton this is Lord Charles Rathbone and Lord Henry Killigrew who are visiting the Colony and have come to inspect the goldfields."

George nodded and only too aware of his grimy fingers did not attempt to shake hands. The two young gentlemen smiled at him, approached the shaft and looked into its depths. It seemed very dark and mysterious down there and rather frightening. George explained the method of working the mine and the two young men thanked him politely and then with Mr Green gingerly walked over heaps of mullock and past abandoned shafts to the track where their horses were waiting. George shook his head for these sort of visitors did not impress him, and went back to the shaft, for he had to think about timbering the bad ground.

No one noticed that when the visitors appeared the Major stepped behind the cart and was busy fiddling with the harness. This was because he knew both the young gentlemen and he felt ashamed to be seen by them, a poor broken man with only one leg, a face marked by too much hard living, too much drink and too much work. One of the young gentlemen was the son of the Duke of Fellshire and the other the son of the Duke of Cleveland. Often he played cards with them at White's and at one time won so much money from Lord Charles that the young man got into serious trouble with his father.

It was midday by the time Mr Green and his noble companions left so Eliza produced pannikins of tea for everyone. George sat on the ground making drawings in the dust with a twig, trying to work out how much timber would be needed for the next twenty feet of the drive. Eliza bent down to hand him his tea and his face was on a level with the neck of her dress where his searching eyes could see the budding shape of two well-formed breasts. She blushed a little and drew back and George averted his eyes. He remembered the incident at the river when her warm body was pressed against his. How she had developed! He had also noticed the way in which the two young lords had looked at her from the corner of their eyes. It made him angry — what right had they?

CHAPTER 19

The summer of the year 1853 was hot and dusty and it was followed by a winter remarkable for rain and cold weather. In May news reached the Turon that the gold regulations were modified. This was a victory for the diggers and the result of the continued agitation by their friends in Sydney. But the hated thirty shillings licence fee was retained. But gone was the double fee for foreigners who now had the same rights as the British subjects. Not that it was very effective, for the Americans said they came from Canada, the French said they were from Quebec and even the Germans had the impudence to say they came from the minute British possession of Heligoland! Clergy- men, teachers and domestic servants were freed from paying the licence and the most hated clause of all, the need for a discharge from one's previous master before a licence would be issued was also gone. But the thirty shillings was looked upon by the diggers as an unjust tax on labour. To the successful digger it was bearable but to the battler scarcely able to make ends meet it was an intolerable burden. The more easily found gold deposits in the river bed were now depleted or covered with water and many diggers left the valley. In Sofala some shops were closed. The diggers were off to Louisa Creek, the Meroo, Tambaroora, the Dirt Holes and so on.

All that winter rain swept the valley, there were bleak winds and once even some snow on the peaks. The Camp was quieter, too. Mr Green came only occasionally from his snug office in Bathurst and it was said that he was soon to leave for England for his health. The day to day work of the field was left to his assistant commissioners and a few troopers. Donald was gone from the service, now installed on his property at King's Plains, immersed in the pleasures of matrimony and the problems of raising sheep. The half company of the Eleventh Regiment tramped back to Bathurst with Lieutenant Ball at its head and then as things remained quiet, back over the Blue Mountains to the flesh- pots of Sydney. The valley of the Turon was quieter than it had been since the first eager diggers found the precious metal in the river gravel.

But Wattle Flat still had its adherents and every month during the winter about five hundred diggers from there took out licences. But, oh, Wattle Flat was back-breaking work, far harder than the alluvial claims. It was a good thing that at least many of the claims were rich. And washing the stuff in the icy river water was painful work in the winter. To stand all day soaked to the waist in water when the temperature was nearly freezing and rain or sleet were falling was work only for real men, for hardened diggers, prepared to work even harder than slaves in search of gold.

The tent George's party lived in during the summer proved too flimsy for winter weather so they built a hut out of rough timber and bark. This kept out the wind and the wet and with a big fireplace with a roaring fire of logs it was possible to keep warm. In the evening in fact with a fire blazing away, a good plate of roast meat before you and a pannikin of tea laced with rum it was cosy, friendly and comfortable. When the meal was finished they would sometimes have a bit of a yarn and George would talk about the old days on the Western Plains and the people he'd met. One evening he remembered there was a copy of David Copperfield in his swag so he got it out and read a chapter aloud.

Other diggers on nearby claims heard about this and asked to be allowed to listen for they were mad about Dickens. So during the winter evenings the hut was crowded with people. George had a good reading voice, although he was pretty taciturn in ordinary conversation but he could read plainly and well without any fancy elocution. By the time the weather grew warmer George was almost at the end of the book and how they all laughed when it turned out that Mr Micawber went to Australia and became a magistrate! This, said the native born, was just what you expected of the Colony. A place where people came when they were not successful in their own country.

In August news came from Sydney that a great meeting was held in the Victoria Theatre to protest against the new Constitution and all the leading liberals and radicals were there. They made long wordy speeches, it seemed, without great significance, but it was the little radical, Deniehy, who really captured the audience's attention with his cutting satirical speech particularly attacking Wentworth's proposal for an hereditary upper house.

"The Botany Bay magnificos, the harlequin autocrats, the Australian mandarins," cried the little man. He suggested that if the Macarthur family received a peerage the coat of arms should be emblazoned with a keg of rum. If Australia was to be favoured with a bunyip aristocracy it would surely bring contempt on the country, he said. This expression caught the fancy of the plebeians and echoed around the diggings. Whenever a man who looked like a gentleman settler rode through the valley the digger would look up from their cradling and say to each other:

"There goes the bunyip aristocracy!"

*   *   *

One day Pat turned up. He came on foot his swag on his back and arrived after dark. He was well enough but he looked tired and a bit grim. Eliza felt that he must have been in some sort of trouble and had come back to lie low for a while. He kept to the claim in daytime and always worked underground. He never went into Sofala, never mixed with other diggers, not even frequented the Wattle Flat inn. No doubt the troopers might take him up over the incident at Erskine Flat but that was a while ago and many of the troopers had gone. Those that remained were too lazy to move out of the Camp. In the evenings when they all sat around the fire and drank rum and tea Pat stayed in his corner and rarely said a word. In the past he always had plenty say, but now he just looked intently at the glowing embers of the fire.

The truth was that he had a lot to think about. For him the struggle for the diggers rights had been the biggest thing in his young life. It showed him there were other things in the world than work. There was comradeship, excitement, stimulation. He'd learned a lot, even a bit of reading and writing and how to talk to people and explain how things were done. In fact some told him he had the gift of the gab. When he fled from the Turon after the big meeting when he knew the traps were at his heels he took refuge at his father's place. This proved pretty dull after Sofala, just hanging around, rounding up his father's cattle now and then or looking for cleanskins in distant gullies. Then his brother Michael came back from Sydney, having served his time Cockatoo Island. Oh, Michael was a real rascal and the prison term had done him no good. In fact now he knew more about cross ways than before he went in. A real rascal and handsome in a true Irish way, well cut chin and nose and black curly hair that the girls liked to get their fingers in and hold on tight. There were one or two married women in the district upon whom he paid visits when their husbands were away. Then one of the husbands came back unexpectedly and there was a fight and Michael arrived home with a black eye and a swollen jaw. He said there was whole clan of Dooleys out looking for him, not only the husband but the brothers as well who wanted to skin him alive.

"Anyhow," he cried. "I'm sick of this place. You might as well be dead as live here!"

So he saddled his horse and rolled his swag.

"Come along with me, lad," he cried to Pat. "Let's get out of here and live a life worth living."

So off they went south before the irate Dooley tribe could catch up with them.

They rode through the thick bush of the mountainous country near the Abercrombie River and frequented dubious shanties that sold bad rum. Michael knew a lot of the people and many hours were spent over noggins yarning with bearded men who appeared to have no specific way of earning a living. One day after Michael and Pat counted the few shillings remaining to them Michael said he knew of a place near Crookwell where the owner, a Mr Brown, kept some grand horses.

"Let's go and bail him up;" said Michael. "We need good horses instead of our knock-kneed nags. There're only two or three men there apart from Brown. No one will stir if we show a gun."

Pat agreed although he knew at the back of his mind that if he asked George or Eliza about it they would have been strongly against. And Michael added that if they got some good horses why shouldn't they go on the road and bail up a coach or two? All sorts of merchants and dealers were travelling the country loaded with gold and banknotes.

"What about the troopers?" asked Pat.

"The troopers! They're only miserable cowardly wretches and they're mounted on old screws even worse than ours."

So one bright morning when Mr Brown was enjoying his breakfast of grilled chops Pat with a handkerchief over his face came through the door and pointed his Colt at the man.

"Bail up, Mr Brown," he said.

Michael went into the kitchen. He only had an old fashioned single shot muzzle loading pistol charged with black powder and fired by a percussion cap. Not much use but suitable for this occasion. The men were having their breakfast and they were rounded up with Mr Brown under Pat's surveillance while Michael went out to the stable where he found three fine bay horses. He bridled and saddled two and put the other on a leading rein and then tied them up at the front of the house. In the dining room where Mr Brown's chops were congealing in their own fat he told the assembled company:

"If any of youse move for half an hour after we've gone I'll come back and cut your gizzards out."

Pat fired a shot through the ceiling to show they meant business. Then they mounted their new steeds and galloped off down the track, the horses moving with the long easy stride of the thoroughbred. Two days later they bailed up a coach near the Towrang Stockade. The passengers tumbled out on the track and showed no resistance, Michael bowed to the women, for he always like to show off to the ladies, and told them he never took anything from a lady that she would not willingly give him, and the younger ones blushed. The men consisted of a couple of squatters going home from Sydney, merchants on the way to the Araluen goldfields and some unidentified but prosperous looking gentlemen. While Michael held them at the point of a new Colt pistol Pat ransacked their pockets and baggage. With three or four gold watches, a couple of new revolvers, a handful of sovereigns and a packet of banknotes the two brothers galloped off to leave the victims commiserating with each other.

Oh, it was a great haul! They were rich! So they rode hard for Fogg's shanty in the Abercrombie where they disposed of the watches to various friends and spent a week carousing. Then they went into Goulburn and fitted themselves out with swell duds at Solomon's store. A few days later they rode into Binda, a tiny village lost-in the bush. They had a drink at the Flag hotel and Michael said:

"Time we did some more work. Now, a coach from Bathurst to Goulburn passes through here every other day. There's one due in this afternoon. We'll bail it up about a mile out of town. There's a couple of troopers stationed there but they've gone to Goulburn to the courthouse today so we've got the place to ourselves."

That afternoon they bailed up the Goulburn coach as it slowed to reach the top of an incline, the horses walking. Michael told the driver to drop his reins and the passengers to alight. Out they came, a couple of squatters, indignant, their wives even more so, two travelling merchants, a hotel keeper and three diggers complete with scarlet shirts, cabbage tree hats, moleskins and blucher boots. They stood there looking angry, their heavy hands dangling by their sides. Pat was all of a sudden aghast. Where had he got himself? Now he was robbing diggers, robbing his mates, the people's he'd worked with! Michael told the passengers to turn out their pockets but when he came to the diggers Pat called out:

"No, not them!"

"Why?" asked Michael, surprised.

"No matter, leave 'em," said Pat forcefully.

Michael shrugged his shoulders, for this was no time to argue. When the loot was collected they mounted and galloped off. At last they camped for the night in the thick scrub and Michael said to his brother:

"What's up with you, Pat? Those diggers had gold on them. Why shouldn't we take it?"

Pat shook his head.

"They're honest fellows who get their money by hard work.

They're not squatters nor storekeepers or publicans. I don't care for them but I won't let me mates be robbed, no I won't have a bar of it."

Michael got into a huff over this for he liked to have his own way. Pat, however, was stubborn. No, he wouldn't take from the diggers, no way. He would rather break up the partnership. Michael, unused to being crossed, said they had better do just that. So off he went to Fogg's shanty while Pat packed his gear and took the road back to the Turon. He sold his horse to a Fish River settler who gave him a poor price but did not ask how such a fine animal came into Pat's possession. Then on foot he walked north to the Turon taking the back road by Lime-kilns where he was less likely to meet people, particularly troopers. It was midday and he went off the track into the bush and boiled the billy and ate salt beef and damper. He stretched out before the fire and puffed his short black pipe while magpies chortled in the trees above. Where lay his future? Pat had no time for squatters and storekeepers but the thought of a life on the road made him uneasy. It might be a gay one for a while but it could end with a rope around his neck. And he was really more interested in the goldfields and the diggers. why not go to Ballarat or Bendigo? In Port Phillip there were thousands and thousands of diggers and a big struggle for diggers' rights was building up, he was told. Perhaps he could play a part in it? He knew how to put the diggers' point of view and people tended to follow the him for that very reason. There might lie his future. But first back to the Turon to lie low for a while, to see his old mates and make a bit of money, and then off to Victoria!

CHAPTER 20

All that winter the claim at Uncle Tom's Hill made money although it was cruel hard work. The Barton party accumulated so much that a wallet of notes was sent off to Mr Lewis's bank for safekeeping. Since his accident the Major seemed to have lost the taste for gambling and Harry, who was also much quieter now, followed his example and both of them began to accumulate dog skin bags full of golden grains.

For the first time that she could ever remember Alice found herself happy and carefree, without a worry for the morrow. She remembered the dream she had long ago in London when the migration agent came to persuade her Eliza to go to Australia. The dream was that she would live in a little cottage with roses around the door. As the time passed she embroidered the dream. There would be a brick path to the front door, a chimney with smoke coming out of it, white curtains at the windows, a pleasant smell of cooking from the kitchen, somewhere a kind husband, perhaps children. It was a dream that had little chance of fulfilment in the grim grey streets of London or even in the sunnier clime of College Street. But now at least she was a step or two nearer. From being a prostitute in a brothel and a kept women, she was now free, not dependent on selling herself to live. The death of the big Vandemonian, she felt, was the real turning point. She had for the first time been able to resist exploitation by a man. She had heard that his dead and rotting body was found in the bush, that his two companions were caught by the police and sent to prison. She felt no pity for them, for they had no pity for her.

Another part of the dream was that Eliza would grow up and marry a good man. For surely this would come true for it was evident that she and George would come together. George was a good man who would respect his wife and not beat her or come home drunk or go off with other women. And when they had finished chasing after gold they would settle down somewhere and have a cottage with roses around the door, too. So the ideas, the vague, wishful, seemingly irrational ideas that had come to her mind in the dim, bleak London slums were coming true, after all. She could scarcely believe it, but it was so.

*   *   *

One day Alice went down the long hill to Sofala for shopping and because someone had told her there was a letter for Harry at the post office. She took the letter back to Wattle Flat to find everyone overjoyed. News was just arrived from Sydney that the licence fee was reduced to ten shillings a month. There was jubilation as the news spread throughout the diggings. All the struggles, all the turmoil were not in vain and the final victory was for the diggers. And the squatters lost for a very good reason. They had hoped to force the diggers back to wages work, but once having tasted the freedom of being one's own master the diggers sought another solution. They took the road to the Victorian diggings by the hundred and the Sydney merchants cursed as they saw the population of the Mother Colony melt away, and with it their trade. So between the diggers' agitation on the one hand and the outraged indignation of the Sydney merchants on the other the Government was obliged to give way and reduce the licence fee.

So at the inn at Wattle Flat and in the hotels in Sofala and the sly grog shanties up and down the river there was great celebration and Parkes, Deniehy and Doctor Lang were toasted over and over again. Now the diggers were free men and the gold was theirs for ten shillings a month. Even the poorer diggers, those who might win only an ounce or two a week, could now afford to take out a licence and not always go in fear of the traps. The next thing, the diggers said to each other, was to break up the squatters' monopoly of the land, for as the gold became more difficult to find, the diggers would need smallholdings to keep themselves and their families.

*   *   *

That evening Alice gave Harry Pole his letter. After he read it and thought for a while in his slow way he went to George and told him that his father was dead. He'd never got on with the old man, he said, and there were rows about money and then trouble with a girl, and that was why he came to the Colony. Now his mother wanted him back to look after the estate and take his place in county society. His mother wrote to say that she would pay his fare, but since he had done so well at the diggings recently he could afford to pay for himself. He shook his head and stammered a little and then he said that he had been very lucky to have fallen in with George, for if he had been by himself he would not have done anything like so well. Then he told the others the news and they shook him by the hand and Eliza brought out the rum bottle for a celebration. A couple of days later they all saw him off on the Bathurst coach and he kissed Eliza and Alice and shook George, Pat and the Major by the hand and promised to write. The driver cracked his whip and the coach was off with Harry waving his hand until he was out of sight. He was gone! Cheerful, empty headed Harry on his way home with a handful of nuggets to show his mother. He was one of the lucky ones, thought Alice. If he had not fallen in with George he would still be working as a wages man and probably spending every penny of his earnings on drink and gambling. Now he was on his way home and would boast to his family of all the exciting things that had befallen him in the Colonies. The Major watched Harry mount the Bathurst coach and disappear down the track southwards. There was sadness in his eyes for he could never take the coach, never board the ship for England, never be welcomed home.

So it was hard work at the mine with three men and a girl and one of the men with a wooden leg. Then the troopers started sniffing around Wattle Flat as if they were looking for someone and Pat decided it was time for him to be off to Victoria. One morning at dawn he shook hands with his friends, patted Rover on the head for the last time, shouldered his swag and disappeared into the bush.

*   *   *

One day the Major and Alice took a cartload of washdirt down to the Turon. The river was running high still and it was a showery day. Every now and then a gust of wind would blow the thin rain down the valley. The Major set up the cradle by the river's edge and filled the hopper with dirt while Alice, wrapped in a warm shawl, dipped a scoop in the river and poured the water over the dirt. The Major picked out the pebbles too large to pass through the openings in the hopper and rocked the cradle gently. It was bleak work but it had to be done.

This went on for a couple of hours. Then as the Major was refilling the hopper with wash dirt his timber stump slipped on a stone and he fell backwards into the river with a splash. He endeavoured to rise but the current caught him and he began to float off downstream. Alice started forward to help him but he slid over a ridge in the gravel and in a moment was whirled away by the fast flowing water: He began to sink and she caught a glimpse of his mouth open in a cry, his arm raised in a call for help. Then he was yards down the river, his head scarcely above water, his arms threshing to keep him afloat. There was no one within easy distance and Alice, aghast, pressed her hands to her head, knowing not what to do. Then she saw that the Major was being carried around a bend in the river and she ran hastily downstream, cutting across the bend to find him swept against the bank, almost at her feet. She climbed out on the roots of a gnarled she-oak and threw him the corner of her shawl, which he managed to catch with one hand. Then began a struggle between Alice and the river which caught and snatched angrily at the Major as if eager to drag him to its depths. Alice took a purchase on the roots with one foot and wound the other end of the shawl around her arm.

"Hold on, hold on!" she cried to the Major who looked at her with despairing eyes as his fingers gradually slipped off the shawl. Bending double Alice leaned over and just caught him by the collar of his coat which at least prevented him from floating away but left Alice panting with exertion. Then the Major was able to take a grip of the roots with one hand and gradually to haul himself upright, and awkwardly to pull himself from the river. At that moment two diggers who had seen from afar what had happened came running up and helped them both onto the bank. They were both exhausted, soaked and shivering. But on the goldfields there was always help for those in trouble and they were taken to a nearby tent, sat in front of a fire and given tea and rum. One of the diggers went off to find the horse and harness the cart. Then after more boiling tea and more rum they were assisted into the cart and told to go home as fast as they could and change their clothes before they caught cold.

That night the Major sank into a deep sleep and dreamed he was riding by a dark stream that flowed down a valley surrounded by bare purple hills. Heavy clouds seemed to press down on him. He rode on and on, his horse's hooves thudding on the dank earth. He looked over his shoulder; something formless and nameless was following him, a presence he could feel but neither hear nor see. He was seized by a terrible fear and he drove his horse wildly forward until the spurs ran with blood and then he felt himself fall into a great pit. He awoke sweating and feverish. Outside the first dim light of dawn was breaking.

He was ill with a fever and it was more than a week before he could get out of bed. One afternoon when George was working and Eliza busy in the kitchen Alice brought him a hot drink. He put the mug down and took both her hands.

"Alice," he said. "You saved my life, for what its worth. I would have been food for the fishes if you hadn't come to my help like that."

She sat down beside him and laid her head on his chest and listened to his heart beating. He stroked her hair. After a few moments he said:

"What am I to do, Alice? The work at the mine is too hard, it's more than I can cope with. I can't go back to England, and I don't want to be a burden on George."

He looked at her despairingly.

Alice had never seen him like that before. He was usually so self composed, so controlled. What must it have cost him to say those few words! Alice pressed his hand.

"Of course you can't go on like this," she said. "But don't worry, we'll find something else, some other way to live."

He lay back in the bed and pressed her hand to his cheek. She had never seen him so low in spirit.

There was a rough inn at Wattle Flat where the Major was in the habit of going for a noggin. When he returned there after his illness the other customers asked him how he felt, if he was better, properly recovered. Rough men slapped him on the back, shouted him a glass of rum and told him to take care of his health.

"Look after yourself, old man," they cried. "Don't go near that river until you're rid of that cough, you're not used to this hard life, like we are."

He suddenly realised that these rough, beared, kindly diggers were sorry for him. He, Major Borlase, late of the Ninth Hussars, whose father had commanded a line regiment at Waterloo, whose family owned an estate in Dorset since the days of Charles the First! Yet to the diggers he was but a poor cripple who occasionally had a drop too much and had to be helped home and who couldn't quite cope with the hard life of the gold digger.

*   *   *

Something had to be done, of course, for things couldn't go on the way they were. It was just not possible for George and the Major to work the mine by themselves. One day the Major came to George and said:

"I can't go on working this way any more, I'm just not up to it and I'd only be a burden on you. So Alice and I have agreed to set up together and take the inn across the way, at Wattle Flat. The woman who owns it, Mrs Flanigan, will sell for a hundred pounds and with what I've got in the bank we'll have enough to pay for it and some left over."

George looked astonished at this while Eliza smiled quietly, for she was party to the secret. Then Alice and the Major went over to see Mrs Flanigan about some details of the purchase and Eliza and George were left alone by the fire. The bush was silent, the profound silence of the Australian forest. George turned to find Eliza looking at him, her eyes wide open, her lips slightly apart. As if drawn by a magnet he went straight to her, took her in his arms and kissed her on the lips, a kiss that sent shivers of fire through his veins.

*   *   *

A couple of weeks later Mr Lewis rode through Wattle Flat on his way to do some banking business in Sofala. He made a detour to Uncle Tom's Hill to see how George was getting on. He found new people on the claim, and the man working the windlass told him that George was away to the Victorian diggings with some new mates, Cornish people, cousins of Henry Treganza, who had a claim down on the river.

"And what happened to his other friends?" asked M: Lewis.

"They've all gone," said the man, a big fair-haired Englishman with a thick West Country accent as he wound up a bucket of dirt and tipped it on the heap.

"The Irish chap, well he went to Victoria earlier because I think the traps were after him. One of the English gents, well he went home and the other's taken the inn at Wattle Flat."

"What happened to the girl?"

"There were two of them in the end," said the Englishman. "One, the elder, married the one-legged chap, and they're at the inn. Eliza married George and is off to Victoria. They were both married at the same time, sort of, at the little chapel at Sofala, by Mr Piddington."

Mr Lewis thanked the man, bade him goodbye and turned his horse on the Sofala track. Well, he thought to himself, I suppose it was inevitable that this would happen. But what will Roland and Amelia say! I can't see little Eliza in Amelia's drawing room. Mr Lewis sometimes found Amelia's pretensions a little aggravating and really not suitable for the general social dispositions of the Colony. Anyhow, there will no doubt be not much communication in the future between the two branches of the Barton family. This was the sort of thing that happened in the topsy-turvy world of the Colony.

At that moment he came out of the bush on the high above Sofala. The township was spread out below him, some rough, ragged gipsy encampment. As rode towards the Prince of Wales

Hotel he reflected on how the glittering grains of gold had turned this empty river crossing a busy little town, how they had brought people from ends of the earth to this once quiet haven in the bush, how they had changed the Colony from a wool and tallow producer into a tumultuous ant heap of people turning world upside down.

END

PLACES IN THE STORY

The places in the story are based on real locations that may be found on current maps.

Sydney. The capital of the autonomous British colony of New South Wales, situated on the sea coast of Eastern Australia at Port Jackson.

Bathurst. First inland town of New South Wales, 120 miles North West of Sydney.

Parramatta. Large settlement fifteen miles on the way from Sydney to Bathurst.

Penrith. Settlement sixteen miles further on the way to Bathurst.

Sofala. Settlement 30 miles north of Bathurst. A centre for gold prospecting in the 1850s. Alluvial gold was found in the banks of the Turon River which winds around Sofala.

Places between Bathurst and Sofala:

Wattle Flat. Three quarters of the way on the road from Bathurst to Sofala.

Limekilns. A small settlement halfway between Bathurst and Sofala.

Winburndale Creek, Mount Clear, Mount Wyagdon, Green Wattle Flat.

Goonigal. Homestead of George Barton, 60 miles West of Bathurst.

The Bogan. district to the North West of Bathurst.

Bald Hills, now Hill End. 40 miles North of Bathurst, another gold mining centre.

Ophir, 30 miles North West of Bathurst, where the first discovery of gold in New South Wales took place in 1851.

Meroo gold field (in central western district of New South Wales).

In Chapter 4:'Loo is short for Woolloomooloo, an impoverished district of Sydney.

In Sofala: A Skillion is a lean-to shed.

PEOPLE IN THE STORY

Chapter 1

Mr Palmer. Church of England clergyman at Sofala.

George Barton. Currency Lad (native born) and bushman. The central character of the story.

Rolly, George's elder brother, gentleman squatter at his Goonigal property in the Bogan district of New South Wales.

Amelia, Rolly's genteel born wife from Sydney.

Ann, Rolly's sister.

Chapter 2

Eliza King. Born in the slums of London.

Alice, Eliza's elder sister. The two young sisters migrate to Australia and end up in the mining settlement of Sofala.

Madame Rose, owner of a brothel in College Street Sydney.

Chapter 3

Goonigal people (George's family in the Bogan district of New South Wales).

Mr Piddington, the dissenting minister in Sofala

Chapter 4

Mr and Mrs Weston, innkeepers in Sofala who employ Eliza.

Chapter 5

Pat Ryan digger mate of George Barton. Militant proto-unionist who accidently kills the government spy Sullivan and goes on the run.

Harry Pole. Eton and Oxford educated. Ineffectual character banished to the colonies who became a digger with George.

The Major. Former British cavalry officer, gambler, fallen on hard times.

Henry Treganza. Cornish miner. Digger mate of George Barton.

Chapter 6

Donald Maclean. The sub-assistant commissioner at Sofala. Local government administrator handling relations with the miners.

Colonel Duncan. Possibly a reference to Major General William Stewart, great grandfather of the author. See "The Claimant" by

Gordon Neil Stewart.
Colonel Duncan's son, Jamie. Possibly a reference to James Horne Stewart, the grandfather of the author and owner of an estate near Bathurst.

Chapter 7
John Murdoch. Irishman partner in firm of McFee. Formerly in a relationship with the prostitute Alice.

Chapter 10
Maria wife of Donald MacClean. Daughter of Jamie Duncan.

Chapter 13
Mr Howson. Could be a reference to the grandfather of the author's first wife, Pamela Hansford Johnson, who toured Australia with a theatrical company before returning to England.

ABOUT THE AUTHOR

Gordon Neil Stewart (25 June 1912 – 15 February 1999) was born in Melbourne into a wealthy Australian family with pastoral interests in the Bathurst district of New South Wales. He was a great grandson of Major General William Stewart (1769–1854) Lieutenant Governor of New South Wales from 1825 to 1827, who after his retirement from the army, settled near Bathurst. Gordon Neil Stewart received a spasmodic education at The Scots College, Sydney due to his parents' frequent travels, but developed a love of reading from long holidays spent in the library of his uncle's house in Bathurst. The family moved to Paris when Stewart was in his late teens. He attended an English language school and then studied art. With other members of his family now based in England, Stewart settled in London where he worked as a journalist and became involved in radical politics. He mixed in literary circles where he met Pamela Hansford Johnson and Dylan Thomas. He is said to have been banished from the poetry circle of Victor Neuburg, a former associate of occultist Aleister Crowley, for making jokes about "yogis and bogeys". In 1936 he married the novelist Pamela Hansford Johnson (1s 1941, 1d 1944) with whom he collaborated on two thrillers under the name Nap Lombard. When the Second World War broke out he joined the British army and served as an officer in the artillery in India, Burma and Indonesia. After his divorce from Pamela Hansford Johnson, Stewart married Doreen Ellen Coulling in 1950 (1d 1952). In 1953 he published "The Cloak and Dollar War", the first book to be written about the Central Intelligence Agency. Intelligence scholar Richard J Aldrich described it as a "revelatory text". Stewart returned to Australia in 1955 and worked in Sydney as a journalist for the mining and construction industry. He retired to Bathurst in 1983 where he wrote and painted. He died in 1999.

OTHER BOOKS BY GORDON NEIL STEWART

The Fight for the Charter (1937, Chapman and Hall).

Blanqui (1939, Victor Gollancz).

Tidy Death (1940, Cassell and Co.) as Nap Lombard with Pamela Hansford Johnson.

Murder's a Swine (1943, Hutchinson) as Nap Lombard with Pamela Hansford Johnson.

Background to new Hungary (1950, Fore publications, London) as Neil Stewart.

Journey to Hungary (1950, Hungarian news and Information Service, London) as Neil Stewart.

The Cloak and Dollar War (1953, Lawrence and Wishart).

Editor: *Australian Stories of Horror and Suspense from the Early Days* (1978, Australasian Book Society) ISBN 978-0-909916-86-2.

House of Bondage (1975, Australasian Book Society) ISBN 978-0-909916-67-1.

Convict rebel: Ralph Entwistle in "Rebels and Radicals" Edited by Eric Fry (1983, George Allen and Unwin, Sydney) ISBN 978-0-86861-285-0.

The Claimant: A story of Australia, Scotland and England. (2019, Harry Stewart). ISBN -13: 978-0-6484929-1-8